Andrew Sperry

Rhyme and reason

Andrew Sperry

Rhyme and reason

ISBN/EAN: 9783337264888

Printed in Europe, USA, Canada, Australia, Japan

Cover: Foto ©Andreas Hilbeck / pixelio.de

More available books at **www.hansebooks.com**

RHYME AND REASON

BY

A. F. SPERRY,

Author of "History of the 33d Iowa."

WASHINGTON, D. C.:
POTOMAC SERIES PUBLISHING COMPANY,
321 Delaware Avenue N. E.
1895.

CONTENTS.

CONTENTS.

JOHN JONES.

A H, Judge, a fine morning! Yes, out for a walk too,
   And just now was wishing for some one to talk to.
Fine lot? You are right; and I safely may say
'Twill be doubled in value a year from to-day,
For Washington's steadily growing, you know,
Even now, though hard times make development slow;
But business is bound to recover, and then
You'll see the whole city just booming again.
It must, for the nation's behind it; and yet
It is equally true, as we should not forget—
Though a quite paradoxical observation—
The city is still behind the nation,
And therefore it clearly must advance
To its proper place when it gets a chance.

   That lot? You're too late: it was recently sold
To a friend of mine here, who proposes to hold
Till he's able to build, if he don't lose his place
In the Treasury. Oh, what a shame and disgrace
To our nation it is that so good men as he
So wholly and always uncertain must be
About their positions! Why, every mere clerk
Ought to know that he's safe while he's doing good work.
And hundreds, yes, thousands—that's none too large—
Would buy property here but for fear of discharge.
And so for the spoils system here we do penance
By making a city of landlords and tenants,
Instead of what otherwise 'twould become,
A city where every man owns his home.

My friend, I believe, is as nearly secure
As anyone now is; at least I am sure
That if merit can strengthen his tenure, he'll stay
Till he wants to resign, or death takes him away.
You'd like him, I'm sure, if you knew him as I do.
For he's one of the very few men you can tie to.
Rare character? Yes, you're felicitous there.
He is one of a class so remarkably rare
That the newspapers speak of it often as *non est*,
Being thoroughly, conscientiously honest;
Not rough, like the commoner "plain, blunt" kind,
But polished in manners, in speech refined;
And yet a certain unconscious air
Bids any who might presume beware
Lest quick resentment should make them feel
That under the polish is solid steel.

No, there's nothing uncommon about his life.
He once loved a woman who isn't his wife;
But that we have most of us done: for it's said
That those whom we first love we seldom wed.
His name? One that many a common man owns:
Euphonious, ample, concise—John Jones.
Euphonious? Yes. Anyhow, I imagine it
Is fully as much so as Richard Plantagenet,
Or Algernon Vavasour Sidney Montgomery,
And just as sufficient, without so much flummery.
Suppose, now, we fancied the name were Italian,
And signified merely some tatterdemalion
With organ and monkey and pitiful story—
Or, better, some popular *primo tenore*—
We'd notice at once, and as if we took pride in it,
How smoothly the vowels and consonants glide in it.
So, just like the natives, who gave, as one reads,
Whole tracts of good land for a few glass beads,
We Americans worship whatever seems foreign to us,
And treat our own good Saxon names as abhorrent to us.

But pardon me, Judge; for I didn't intend
To rattle on so when I spoke of my friend.
A real estate agent, alas! is but human—

And it does rest one's brain so to talk like a woman!
Tell you more about John?   Well, please give me a light.
Can I talk while I smoke? Yes, from morning till night.

We were born the same day—some few summers ago.
His parents were poor—"poor but pious," you know.
They moved to Wisconsin while John was quite small;
And he worked on the farm in spring, summer and fall,
And in winter attended the public school:
For in those days that was the general rule
In those pioneer, far-away Western communities;
But he made the best use of his scant opportunities,
And, beside his mere book-educational gains,
Learned one thing still better—to use his own brains;
And though no one can hope to in all things excel,
Yet whatever John did he did thoroughly well.
At eighteen he was sent to a neighboring town
Where a sort of high school, of some local renown,
Gave a chance his expenses by labor to pay.
'Twas the best he could do: he must make his own way:
And he studied and worked; and whatever he learned
Stuck by him the better for being self-earned.

So two years, or thereabouts, passed, when there came
To the town a young lady, Miss Mason by name,
Who lived in Detroit, but whose folks sent her there
To visit some friends, and breathe pure country air—
Ostensibly that, but in fact, I suppose,
To get her away from the fast city beaux.
She was handsome and lively, just turning nineteen,
And a natural nestler. Don't know what I mean?
Well, of all the devices of feminine art,
The surest to capture a strong man's heart
Is this of the nestler, who presses her face
To his breast as a safe, fond resting-place.
Why, I think, if my landlady even—confound her!—
Should try it on me, my arms would go 'round her
Impulsively, yes, and against my will,
Though it meant an advance on my next month's bill,
And I knew it beforehand. Well, this Miss Mason
Knew all of the notes in the whole diapason

Of flirting, and played them with skill and grace;
And so, with her style and her handsome face,
She turned all the young men's heads, except
John Jones's; but he persistently kept
His mind on his books, and thought, as afar
He saw her the central social star
Before which all other stars grew dim,
Such beauty and grace were not for him.
He was poor; he couldn't even afford
To wear good clothes; and he worked for his board.
She would not even speak to such as he;
So he thought: but how different things may be
From what we expect! She saw him one night
At a party, and noticed, as well she might,
That he seemed a young man of brains and breeding,
In looks and in manners far exceeding
The most of those there who were better dressed;
And at once to a friend a wish she expressed
To become acquainted; and so they met,
By a very strange chance, he thought—and yet
Since then I have heard him express a doubt
If in all this world, were the truth found out,
A single event, no matter how small,
Ever had any chance about it at all.

But they met, at any rate. Well, you know
How fast acquaintances sometimes grow.
In a month or two it began to be noted
That Jones and Miss Mason were quite devoted,
And "Love at first sight" was frequently quoted.
In this case, too, 'twas at least half right,
For first love most often is love at first sight.
It was John's first attack; and his great sincerity
Of character gave it increased severity.
He never was one to do things half-way;
And so, very naturally, one day
When he and Miss Mason returned from a walk,
And, just at the proper turn of the talk,
And with just the most sweetly artless grace,
She nestled up to him and pressed her face

To his breast, he gave her a strong embrace,
And love's passionate story burst from his tongue
Like a torrent. Ah!—Well, we once were young,
And we know how it was; but we never knew
What we said at the time, for men never do.
They remember each word, each look and tone
Of the lady, but can't recall their own.

It's sure enough, though, that John made an end
Of his speech by declaring it must depend
On her definite answer, there and then,
Whether he were most happy or wretched of men.
That's the way with first love: life's weal or woe
All hung on a woman's yes or no.
It's by later experience men are taught
There are fish in the sea good as ever were caught;
And John never thought of that then. With a sigh
He released her, and waited for her reply.

"Well, really," she said, in the calmest of tones,
"You flatter me highly indeed, Mr. Jones.
Believe me, I certainly didn't intend
Our pleasant acquaintance so quickly to end.
You've been very polite and attentive, just such
A companion as I always like very much;
But pardon me, please, if your feelings I hurt
When I own I have merely been playing the flirt.
I like you; indeed, I'm not sure I don't love you;
But my station in life has been somewhat above you.
My tastes are expensive. You cannot support
A wife quite so cheap as a girl you may court.
I never could live on mere kisses and honey:
If I marry at all, I shall mary for money."

The blow was a hard one. John sank in a chair,
And a moment or two sat silently there
With his head in his hands. This world, once so fair,
Seemed suddenly black with the gloom of despair.
Then he rose to his feet. His face was white,
His jaws set hard, and his lips drawn tight.
He stepped to the door, took his hat, put it on,

Said "Good-bye, Miss Mason." bowed, and was gone.
That was all. But if this had appeared on the stage
Instead of in life, just imagine what rage,
What striding around, and gesticulation,
There'd have been, to "develop the situation!"
The stage "holds the mirror to Nature," they say;
But I tell you, Judge, it don't work that way
As a matter of fact, at least not for us
Americans. We don't make much fuss.
We are undemonstrative, silent men
In trouble or danger. Why, time and again
I have seen our wounded soldiers lying
On the field of battle, bleeding, dying
In agony, helpless though not alone;
But I rarely heard one even groan.
And many a time, in wild Western life,
I have seen the beginning of deadly strife,
When, though nerves were at tension and pulses quick,
All the noise didn't drown the revolvers' click.

Well, John left the school and went back to the farm,
And worked like a man for whom life has no charm,
Till the war broke out, when at once he enlisted
As a private soldier; and that's where he missed it;
For things were then in such a condition
That he might just as well have had a commission;
But he thought it was duty's call he heeded,
And that men with muskets were then most needed.
So he went as a private, and saw hard service,
Of the kinds that try just what a man's nerve is.
Wherever our Regiment went, he was there,
And for duty, and always got his share,
And did it faithfully, and at last
Came home all right when the war was past.
Not crippled? No. Don't look so astounded:
There are many brave soldiers who never were wounded.
I knew a man once who came home from the war,
After four years' service, without a scar,
Though in thirteen regular battles he'd been;
And he died at last from the prick of a pin.

That's Fate—but let's drop that subject now:
We know that it is so, but can't know how.

No, John wasn't promoted; I can't say why,
But perhaps because he never would try
To obtain promotion. Remember, then
We had something over a million of men
As mere private soldiers. There had to be
More privates than officers then, you see;
And John's not the only one I've met
Who isn't even a Captain yet.
But our life in the army was like the stuff
The photographers use to develop the rough
And fleeting impression the sun has made
On the plate, to a picture that will not fade:
For some a blessing, for others a curse;
Making some men better and others worse;
But John, like the most, I believe, of those
Who returned from the war, whether friends or foes,
Is a wiser, better and nobler man
Than he was when his soldier life began.

Well, after the war he went into trade,
And slowly but surely and steadily made
His way in the world; and he met and loved
And won a woman who since has proved
For him the greatest blessing in life,
A loving, faithful and sensible wife—
Not one of those merely female creatures
Consisting entirely of form and features
And not knowing enough to go in when it rains,
But a whole human being, including the brains—
Not handsome, perhaps, but at least good-looking,
Plump, healthy and jolly, and skilled in cooking
As well as piano-pounding, in fact
As able and ready to think and act
As her husband is. Yes, such women as she
Are as worthy to vote as a man can be,
And ought to have equal rights with men
In every respect; and they'll have them when
The world gets wise enough. Wait till then.

Well, well! How I spin! But there's not much more
To be told. In the summer of '84
Their first and only great trouble came,
When they saw all their property vanish in flame
And themselves in an hour from prosperity hurled
Out homeless and penniless into the world.
And then—but it's hardly worth while to relate
How it happened, or rather, was ordered by fate,
That while he was looking for permanent work
He was offered a place as a Treasury clerk.
They have been here since then; and both he and his wife
Think this is the happiest part of their life;
And indeed I believe they have more real pleasure
Than some people have whose purses will measure
Far more than John's; for with ease a cent
Is more than a dollar with discontent.

But what of Miss Mason? Oh, nothing uncommon.
She married for money at last, poor woman!
And got it, but with it a worthless curse
Who was born for a fool but had made himself worse
By drinking; and though they were married in style,
And lived in high luxury too, for a while,
Yet soon he began to neglect and ill-treat her,
And even, when drunker than common, would beat her.
She lost all her beauty, and with it her health,
While in spreeing and gambling he squandered his wealth.
Till in less·than ten years he had spent it all,
And was killed in a low-life drunken brawl;
And the widow, with two little girls to be fed,
Had to·take in washing to earn their bread;
But she didn't mourn much when she heard he was dead,
For she'd thought many times since her troubles began,
How much better 'twould be to have married a man.
At length, a mere wreck of what once she had been,
Grown old prematurely, and haggard and thin,
By the kindness of friends whom she formerly knew
She was given a Government clerkship too,
And drifted here that way, as other wrecks do.

Has John seen her yet, since she came here? Yes,

Just once; and he told me he couldn't guess
Who the lady might be whom he happened to meet
One Sunday while strolling along the street,   [name.
And who stopped, looked astonished, and called him by
At first he suspected some confidence game,
And was coldly polite; but she seemed to desire
Just a talk; and, not waiting for him to enquire,
Told who she once was, and her story related
In outline and substance as I have just stated.
Her motive, John said, he could only surmise;
And indeed he was so overcome with surprise
That he asked no questions, as she asked none;
And not till she'd told him good-bye, and passed on,
And some other person had met him and spoken,
Was the spell of bewilderment finally broken.
Then, absurdly enough, to his mind it came
That she hadn't told him her present name,
And so he could hardly find her again
If he wished; and they've never met since then.

"But had you," I asked him, "no thoughts, no feeling,
While she her sad story was thus revealing?"
"Thoughts? Yes," he answered, "an endless host;
But what I seem now to remember most
Was a feeling as if I were seeing a ghost."
"But," said I, "when she mentioned her once-loved name
Did it kindle no spark of the former flame?"
And he smiled, and for answer asked me to scratch
A light for my pipe with a burned-out match
That he happened to see. Then he suddenly turned
To a serious talk; and I very soon learned
There were depths in his nature which never before
I had guessed, though for twenty-five years or more
We've been intimate friends. But who ever has known
The heart of another—or even his own?

Well, candidly, Judge, I could hardly guess
Whether John would consider his life a success
Or not. Ambitions he's had, I suppose,
As all of us have them; but nobody knows,
For he never complains; he just does his best,

And trusts to the Lord for all the rest.
He thinks, indeed—and so does his wife—
That the true intention of human life
Is self-development, and the test
Is whether one makes the most and best
He can of himself; and if this is true,
They're all right, for that's certainly what they do.
So, taking this into consideration,
And knowing that each of us has his station
In life determined by various causes
Outside of himself, and that one of Fate's laws is
That some must be greater and others less,
I cannot but think his life is a success.
At any rate, Judge, when the world you scan,
And reflect how rare is an honest man,
And how fitly called God's noblest work,
Though even an unknown Government clerk,
Or whatever his station in life may be,
You'll easily pardon to one like me
The pride and pleasure with which he owns
The acquaintance and friendship of plain John Jones.

Ah, thanks for the compliment! Yes, I will;
And you'll find that he thoroughly fills the bill.
What! Nine already? How time does fly!
Well, I hope you've enjoyed it as well as I,
And here is your stopping-place? Well, good-bye.

FOG AND PHILOSOPHY.

Some years ago, as I have heard related
   By men whose looks and size
   Were such that we young people deemed it wise
Never to question anything they stated,
   Upon his own ancestral ground,
   In old Connecticut, close by the Sound,
Lived Deacon Gray,
   A sober, upright man,
   After the standard old New England plan
Established in an earlier, sterner day.
   He never laughed aloud;
And if at some rare interval a smile
   Lit up his face, like sunshine on a cloud,
It lasted but a very little while.
   Utilitarian of the strictest school,
   Hard-headed, shrewd and cool,
He was as purely matter-of-fact,
Methodical, exact,
   And void of sentiment as a two-foot rule.

Let me observe right here,
It always seemed to me a little queer
   That such a very singular circumstance
As this which I'm proceeding to relate
Should happen in that sober, steady State,
   And by strange chance,
Or by still stranger fate,
   To such a man as good old Deacon Gray.

But be this as it may:
Truth even more strange than fiction's said to be;
And I but tell the tale as it was told to me.

Full fifty years the Deacon's barn had stood,
Entirely sound and good;
For it was built of solid wood,
    With careful skill and honest work,
    Such as in these sad days of sham and shirk
One seldom sees.
Its massive beams, hewn from the straightest trees,
    Looked as if meant to last forevermore;
    And its great mows and bins held ample store
    Of hay and grain, while on the central floor
The farm utensils all found shelter,
Not stowed in helter-skelter,
    But ranged in order; and outside of all,
    In the low sheds, each to its proper stall,
The cattle learned to come at night together,
    Needing no other call
Or warning than the stern New England weather.

So for full fifty years the barn remained,
Still growing rougher and more weather-stained.
    But needing no repairs, until one day,
After a steady rain for near a week,
    The Deacon found his hay
Was wet because the roof had sprung a leak.
    Now this would never do, of course;
    And so he harnessed up his horse
And went to town that very day
    And bought the nails and shingles, and at night
Made preparations to begin the work
    With the next morning's earliest light.

    This, please to bear in mind,
Was long before we had a weather clerk
    To sort out weather just as we're inclined.
In those old days,
    Before our Modern Science got a name
And won so much self-praise,

They had to take the weather as it came.
But Deacon Gray had read
That passage of the Scripture where 'tis said,
    Whoso regards the clouds, he shall not sow;
Whoso observes the winds, he shall not reap;
    And he had come to know
The hidden wisdom those old maxims keep.

And so, at morning's earliest dawn,
    Or rather, it its time for dawning,
Straight of bed he jumped, without a yawn—
    He never wasted time in idle yawning—
And straightway went out-doors
To do the morning chores,
    And found the fog so dense,
    He couldn't see the nearest fence;
Indeed, he couldn't even see the ground,
So thick the fog rolled in from old Long Island Sound.

Emblem of human life is such a day!
    We grope about
    With hesitation and in constant doubt
Because we cannot see our way.
    Surrounding objects dimly we perceive,
    But nothing of the future. We believe,
Taught by experience, that what has been
Will be again;
    And so,
Moment by moment only, we exist,
    While most of what we most desire to know
Is shrouded in impenetrable mist.

But Deacon Gray had no such fancies;
    He saw no poetry this life adorning
And with its incidents and circumstances
    Continually mingling;
For him it was a very foggy morning,
    And nothing more. It would not stop his shingling,
And that was all he thought of then.
So, after breakfast, out he went again,

And climbed up on the barn, and straight began,
    According to his plan,
Nailing the new pine shingles, smooth and white,
Upon the roof. He worked with all his might,
    And thought of nothing else; and so time passed
    Unnoticed, till at last
The first faint gleam of sunshine o'er him hovered,
And then he suddenly discovered
    That he had made a very strange mistake—
    So strange, indeed, that I would hardly make
This statement merely on my own authority.
    I only say
    That I have heard it made in just this way
By men whose physical superiority
    Compelled restraint
From any visible sign of doubt
    When they avowed, by every saint
In the most comprehensive catalogue,
    That Deacon Gray had shingled out
Fifteen or twenty feet upon the fog!

Just here the story always ended,
    Abruptly, I confess,
    Leaving the hearer free to guess
Whether the Deacon still remains suspended,
Or whether he descended
    Abruptly also. But I've often thought
    That one who looks at matters as he ought
Might find occasion
Sometimes to use it as an illustration.

For instance, take a modern craze.
It has been known since prehistoric days
    That what we call the mind
    Has some strange powers, uncertain, undefined,
Beyond its customary sphere;
    But all that has been written, said or sung
    Since Greece and Rome were young
Has never made this truth one whit more clear;
    And nothing have we gained
By all the experiences of human history

Toward better knowledge of the mystery,
    Or toward the hope of having it explained.
'Tis like the fatal Pole
For which so many a daring soul
    Has bravely sailed,
    In hope to find it though all others failed,
And perished mid eternal ice and snow:
We know the Pole is there, and that is all we know.
So when my wife, a "mind cure" convert, preaches
    Her new belief, this so-called "Christian Science,"
    In which she has just now such firm reliance—
Unconscious utterly that what it teaches
    Is merely some old notions with new names—
And proves it all by some preposterous yarn,
    Her loving husband tenderly exclaims,
"At it again, eh!—shingling off the barn!"

And Modern Science, too, so called—
    Not Christian science, but the opposite—
In Truth's bright sunlight overhauled
    Would often prove this illustration fit:
So many of its vain Professors seem
    Extremely anxious to believe
Christianity an idle dream,
Or merely man-made scheme
    Intended to deceive.
Wilfully blind,
Persistently determined not to find
    A Great First Cause,
    Author and Arbiter of nature's laws,
They yet accept
    With eager, credulous haste
Alleged discoveries which they hope may show
The Bible records wrongly kept
    And Bible dates erroneously placed.
    Of the Pierian spring they've had a taste;
And what they merely think, they think they know.
    So when some self-styled Scientist displays his
    Omniscience in long words and sounding phrases,
But takes mere theories and hypotheses

For solid facts, I listen, ill at ease
    But humbly silent, to his monologue,
    And think meanwhile, "Young man, you're shing-
        ling on the fog."

Religion too, alas!
    Has doctrinaires and dogmatists, who preach
Their man-made creeds and forms as God's own law;
And the too-credulous mass,
    Impressed by ex-cathedra modes of speech,
Listens with undiscriminating awe.
    Yet nevertheless,
    When these self-chosen oracles profess
More knowledge of God's purposes and ways
    Than He saw fit
In the Apostles' days
    Alike to all men to reveal,
    As now recorded in His Holy Writ,
The humblest hearer in the synagogue
    Should know and feel
That they are merely shingling on the fog.

Law too, and medicine, politics, the press,
    And almost every other occupation,
Give frequent opportunities to express
    By this brief metaphor the situation.
In short, whenever anyone mistakes
    New words and phrases for new information,
Or bare assertion for the truth, or makes
    Mere theorizing serve for explanation,
Or dogma for religion, or forsakes
    Sound common sense for hare-brained speculation,
He seriously errs, in just the way
    That calls to mind, as fitting illustration,
The sad predicament of Deacon Gray.

Love's Young Dream.

When first we feel the influence
    Of Love's delicious dream,
All Nature's beauties newly dressed
    In brighter colors seem;
The inward joy reflects itself
    On everything around;
Our life is love, and joy and hope
    And happiness abound.

Like magic glass, our dazzled eyes
    Will magnify each charm
Of her we love, and paint them all
    In colors rich and warm.
The rosy cheeks, the flowing hair,
    The eyes so bright and clear,
Have each a special beauty and
    Enchantment ever dear.

The winning smile, the joyous glance,
    Those moments pure of bliss
When the soul dissolves in ecstacy
    And melts into a kiss—
O, with thrilling rapture ever will
    Their memory with us stay,
And half supply their places when
    Themselves are far away.

If this ecstacy be dreaming,
    While illusion is delight
Let us cherish and enjoy it,
    Ere it vanish from our sight.
Let us revel in its beauty;
    Let us bid the spell remain.
If this ecstacy be dreaming
    Let us never wake again.

The Choice.

Waubun, the Sachem, feeling rather grum,
One day set out alone the woods to roam;
And toward the Sacred Cave he wandered slow,
Where none before had ever dared to go;
When lo! a fragrant smoke, out-issuing far,
Filled with delicious perfume all the air.
It wrapped the Sachem like a fairy veil,
Stealing his senses; and to earth he fell.

When he awoke, 'twas in the Spirit Land;
And all around him sat a solemn band
Of ghostly braves who'd passed to t'other side
Of Charon's ferry. They were all supplied
With calumets, and smoked, and showed Waubun
What 'twas they smoked, and how the thing was done,
And bade him, when he saw his tribe again,
Give this new knowledge to deserving men,
And they should find a comforter indeed,
To soothe their sorrows, in the fragrant weed.

Thus from above began tobacco's sway.
And when our good forefathers came away
From dear old England to this savage shore,
Freedom attracted some, tobacco more;
And most for this they tilled the fertile soil,
And most this harvest recompensed their toil.
Yet still full happiness was seldom seen,
For wives, alas! were few and far between.
Tobacco ruled the market rather high:
Why not more wives with their tobacco buy?
Happy the thought! So easily 'twas done,
The next ship brought a wife for every one.

With me the case is different. Fate decreed
That I should lose a wife to save the weed.
After she'd promised to be mine till death,

She smelled the fragrant odor in my breath,
And straightway on me laid the dread command,
"Resign tobacco or resign my hand."
Brief was the struggle. 'Tis enough to say,
She's a grass-widow, and I smoke to-day.

———o———

The Old Love in the New.

Yes, when I was young—like some long-vanished vision
 'It seems as I muse on those memories dear,
Or like glimpses again of the glories Elysian
 We knew ere we came to this sorrow-cursed sphere—

I loved a fair maiden with purest devotion;
 We were pledged to each other till life should be o'er;
And when her dear form sank to rest in the ocean,
 I thought my crushed heart could feel pleasure no more.

But years rolled around, and diminished my sorrow—
 Youth's pains, like its pleasures, pass quickly away—
And Hope now from Memory magic will borrow,
 As lost love revives in a new one to-day.

Yet think me not faithless to Memory's treasures:
 Our fate and our purposes seldom agree;
And love now awakes for me youth's dearest pleasures,
 Which forever had slept but tor meeting with thee.

———o———

A Memory.

There will come sometimes, with a magic power,
 A thought of the buried Past;
I remember each rosy, happy hour
 Of a bliss too sweet to last.

I think of each walk in the lonely grove,
 By the side of the placid stream,
With the maiden my young heart learned to love;
 And they seem to me now as a dream.

Those plighted vows, that mutual kiss,
    That wealth of love divine—
Could I wish to live over an hour, 'twere this,
    The hour when I called her mine.

But life's bitterest draught I have had to drink,
    To the dregs of its deepest woe;
And so of the silent Past I think,
    And the days of long ago.

———o———

Parting.

When I am gone, who will regret,
    Or give a passing thought to sorrow?
Will lips that smile so sadly yet
    But laugh the merrier to-morrow?

Will he who takes my hand to-day
    With clasp so fond of friendship seeming,
To others, thoughtless, turn away
    While absent I of him am dreaming?

And she whose love has been to me
    My little all on earth of heaven—
Shrined in her bosom shall I be,
    With love as true as first 'twas given?

Friends, friends, with streaming eyes I part
    From your loved circle. Time may sever
The ties that bind another's heart,
    But mine is bound to you forever.

———()———

A Translation of Virgil's Fourth Eclogue.

A loftier strain, O Pastoral Muse, than thine
We sing: not all admire thy humble line.
If rural subjects in our verse appear,
They must be worthy of a Consul's ear.

The final age of Sybil song is found,
And Time begins anew his mighty round.
The virgin Justice now returns again—
The golden age of Saturn's happy reign.
Now doth an offspring new from heaven descend,
And first with him this barbarous age shall end;
With him, to all that spreads beneath the skies,
A glorious age, the golden era, rise.
Oh, chaste Lucina, guard the infant child:
Thy own Apollo reigns, O goddess undefiled.

Thou, Pollio, thou this glorious age shalt see
Begun while Rome is governed still by thee.
The mighty times foretold shall then begin,
Even in thy rule; and all that may remain
Of all our errors, every lingering trace
Of all the wrongs and evils of our race,
Shall fade, and free the world from endless fears.
Then thou, O child, shalt live celestial years,
See heroes mingling with the friendly gods,
And they behold thee in their blest abodes;
Behold thy peaceful realm the world embrace,
And thee adorned with all thy father's grace.

For thee, O child, the grateful earth shall pour
The early fruits spontaneously she bore;
With wandering ivy, spikenard sweet be seen,
Acanthus smiling, and the Egyptian bean;
The tender kids with milk the fold shall cheer,

And largest lions wake no more their fear;
Thy very cradle shall around thee shower
Each fragrant herb and every pleasing flower;
No more with venom shall the serpent swell,
Nor poisonous herb deceitful death distill;
But everywhere instead the graceful shape
Shall spring of Syria's aromatic grape;
At once the glorious deeds of sire and son,
Judging their merits, thou shalt look upon;
On barren fields the golden grain shall bend,
From brambles rude the blushing grape depend,
And from the oak's wide-spreading branches all
The dewy drops with honied sweetness fall.

Yet some few traces of the old disgrace
May still remain, which drove our hapless race
In hollow ships to tempt the treacherous main,
Fence towns with walls or plow the furrowed plain;
And from these stains ere yet the world is clear,
New Typhys shall, and other Argos, bear
Their chosen heroes, other wars destroy,
And new Pelides rage before another Troy.

But when thy manhood's years, O child, shall come,
The wandering merchantman no more shall roam,
Nor naval pine the wares of commerce bring,
For everywhere shall earth bear everything:
The soil no more the rending plow shall feel,
No more the vineyard dread the pruning steel;
The hardy plowman then shall lay aside
The oxen's yoke; no more the fleece be dyed,
But grazing sheep to change their color learn,
And purple now or golden yellow turn;
Even in the fields the tender lambs shall know
In purest white or red of dazzling hue to grow.

This age the agreeing Fates, in fixed decree.
Have woven in their web of destiny.
O, haste, ye happy times, ye glorious days!
The hour has come, the passing moment stays.

Receive the mighty honors from above,
O loved of gods, O great increase of Jove!
Bowed down with shame the guilty world is found,
Land, sea and sky, and all the sun goes round;
But, freed by thee, then shalt thou all behold
Pure and rejoicing in that age of gold.

Oh, could but length of days enough be mine,
Enough of soul to sing thy deeds divine,
Not Thracian Orpheus should my strain excel,
Not Linus' self should wake the song so well,
Though with their aid paternal to them given,
Apollo, Calliopea, came from heaven;
With me contesting even should Pan aspire,
E'en he, Arcadia judge, should own his vanquished lyre.

O, glad, sweet boy, thy mother with a smile:
For thee her pangs she bore a weary while.
O, haste, sweet boy; for whom no parent greets,
Him to his board of rich, ambrosial sweets .
No god deems ever worthy to be led,
Nor goddess to the honors of her bed.

———O———

Beyond the clouds, beyond all doubt and fear,
Even as the pure light of the stars above.
Not dazzling but serenely bright and clear
Forever, fadeless, changeless—thus our love.
God grant His blessing on our mutual life,
And make me worthy thee, my own true-hearted wife!

The Demon of the Whirlwind.

The air is strangely still.
  The Sabbath evening sun
Sinks slow, as if against his will
  He left the earth alone.

And lo! in the darkening west
  A deeper gloom appears.
The Prince of the Powers of the Air confessed
  His terrible form uprears.

His spreading wings unfurled
  A shadowy horror seem.
His voice of thunder shakes the world,
  And his eyes in lightnings gleam.

He mounts on the wings of the wind,
  While the clouds their torrents pour.
Gloom, ruin and death he leaves behind,
  And destruction goes before.

In horrid glee he sings
  On his throne-cloud rolling black.
While his airy legions flap their wings
  And speed on their terrible track:

"Ho, ye cities and temples and towers,
  Uplifted in all your pride,
Ye shall fall: too long have your vaunted powers,
  Unpunished, my rule defied.

"Now, now is your day of doom;
  Ye shall feel no feeble gale:
The Prince of the Powers of the Air is come,
  And your boasted strength shall fail.

"And ye mortals of human race,
  I will scatter ye like the chaff;
I will mock at the woe on every face;
  At your terror will I laugh.

"Will ye try my realm again?
  Will ye sail my seas of blue?
Aye, ye shall; but the living shall weep the slain,
  And their tears shall fall for you.

"Your halls of pomp and pride
  I will tumble about your heads.
See, once where they rose on every side,
  My wrath their ruin spreads.

"Ha, ha! ye puny things!
  Do I freeze your blood with fear?
Do ye cower in the gloom of my shadowy wings,
  And my voice of thunders hear?

"Aye, fall on your knees in prayer;
  Remember your Maker now:
Even while ye pray your souls are there,
  And before Him in judgment bow."

Exulting thus he sings,
  A terror in every tone;
And at every sweep of his horrid wings
  Is heard a dying groan.

Thus is his vengeance done;
  And o'er the frightened plain,
As the Demon flies in his fury on,
  Gloom, ruin and death remain.

"O, Father and God above,
  Give ear to our feeble prayer!
Look down on us, in Thy infinite love,
  And help us in our despair!

"Oh, save us from further harm;
    Let our prayers be not in vain!
Make bare, O Father, Thy mighty arm,
    And the Demon's rage restrain!"

Thus to our God we prayed;
    And His arm deliverance bore:
The Demon's awful course was stayed,
    And his wrath destroyed no more.

In trembling notes of joy,
    To God our praise we sing.
Awhile may a demon's rage destroy,
    But He will deliverance bring.

Yet long shall each faithful heart
    For the dead its vigils keep:
And oft shall the manly tear-drop start,
    And woman in silence weep.

And oft shall our children hear
    The tale of horror told,
And pray they may never know such fear
    As their fathers felt of old.

———()———

Parting Hymn.

Brothers, sisters, we must part
    Ere shall come another day.
Though your converse glads the heart,
    Duty calls: we must away.

Pleasant hours we here have known,
    Closer ties of friendship formed;
Round our path fresh flowers have grown,
    And our souls new fervor warmed.

Soon, these pleasant hours gone by,
    Shall our hearts, in secret pain,
Ask, as memory brings the sigh,
    "When shall we all meet again?"

Let us pray, as we go forth,
    Each his way, that grace be given
So to do our work on earth
    That we all may meet in heaven.

————()————

The Voice of the One we Love.

O, sweet is the voice of the birds that sing
    As joyous at morn we roam,
And sweet is the hum of the wild bee's wing
    As he seeks his flowery home.

And the viol and lute and the soft guitar
    May tender emotions move;
But there is a music sweeter far:
    'Tis the voice of the one we love.

At its lightest sound, the lover's heart
    A tender thrill will own;
And in words of love when the sweet lips part,
    There is bliss in every tone.

Then tell me no more of the harp and lute,
    Though sweet their music be:
Thy voice, my love, though all else were mute,
    Is music enough for me.

————()————

In an Album.

As one who, wandering to some well-known spot,
   Some sacred place to memory ever dear.
Inscribes his name, which else had been forgot,
   As if to say "Lo, I too once was here,"
And seeks to save his memory by a line
Of feeble worship at the hallowed shrine.

So seems he now who, soon, perhaps, to part
   From one whom he has learned to so esteem,
Leaves here an humble tribute from the heart,
   In hope that she for whom he writes may deem
One thought not ill-bestowed upon his name,
Who, having this, could wish no better fame.

———O———

The Lover's Life.

Who can tell the lover's life—
   Hope to-day, despair to-morow:
Blissful, torturing, constant strife
   'Twixt unbounded joy and sorrow!

Then, if love be unreturned,
   All his hopes one cold word dashes,
And the heart whose passion burned
   Like a furnace, turns to ashes.

———O———

"Turn Away those Strange, Soft Eyes."

"Turn away those strange, soft eyes:
    They oppress me with their beauty;
And the light that in them lies
    Lures me far from right and duty."

Never eyes so bright as thine
    Shone with such a depth of feeling—
Like the diamond in the mine,
    All its hidden wealth revealing.

Take away the witching spell
    Those dark eyes have thrown around me!
Loving thee alone were well,
    But another's love hath bound me.

Yet in vain is Duty's call,
    Vain her feeble, fond endeavor:
Love alike will vanquish all—
    Dearest, I am thine forever.

———()———

Saturday Night.

As the miner, down in his living tomb,
    Toils cheerfully day by day,
Where the fresh air of heaven ne'er can come,
    Nor ever a sunlight ray,
What buoys his spirit up so well
    And keeps his heart so light?
Ah, Hope and Memory, yours the spell—
    'Tis the thought of Saturday night,
When the dear ones all whom he loves so well
    Shall bless his Saturday night.

And so, as I toil the long days through,
  Till their wearisome round is past,
There will come the thought of an hour with you
  That may crown the week at last;
And my heart is cheered to the work once more,
  And the star of Hope grows bright,
As I think of the hours that have gone before,
  And then, next Saturday night,
When an hour, my darling, with you once more
  May bless my Saturday night.

—()—

Love of Wisdom.

Wisdom came to me one day,
  Clad in robe of spotless whiteness;
Round her head, in radiant play,
  Dazzling beams of heavenly brightness.

Grace and purity and truth
  Shone in every glance upon me;
Fadeless beauty, endless youth—
  These the charms by which she won me.

Yet, though all my soul was thrilled
  With unutterable yearning,
Still it seemed in fetters held,
  Still to things of earth returning.

Oh, this nature, all too base
  To receive the proffered blessing!
Wisdom so I can but praise,
  Loving still, but ne'er possessing.

Love's Birthplace.

As, ever constant through all changes,
    Though oft of other climes it learns,
Yearly, wherever else it ranges,
    The bird of passage still returns
To that dear spot where first the light
It saw, and first began its flight,

So turns my soul, or glad or weary,
    As joys or sorrows rule the hour,
From scenes of mirth or prospects dreary,
    To the unchanged, familiar bower
Where first that highest joy it proved
Of loving and of being loved.

———o———

To Mary.

On the Dead Sea's dreary shore,
    As the lonely traveler, turning,
Views the waste of desert o'er,
    Nought of life or joy discerning,

Sudden, with delighted eyes,
    Sees the desert-apple blooming
Like a flower of Paradise,
    Seeming all the air perfuming,

Gazing then not long he stands;
    Heedless through the thorns he dashes,
Plucks the fruit with eager hands,
    Tastes—and finds but dust and ashes.

Mary, so, when first we met,
   On my waste of life, thy seeming
Bloomed upon my soul, as yet
   Little of its future dreaming.

Now, though still thy form must live
   Where I once but joyed to place thee.
Half my life I'd freely give
   Could I from the rest erase thee.

———()———

Yearnings.

Filled with the rarer, lighter breath of heaven.
   Sailing majestic through the upper sky,
Yon silken globe, now to the free winds given,
   Far in the distance dim floats proudly by.

A thing of conscious life and grace it seems,
   Exulting in existence; such a being
As often we have pictured in our dreams,
   When airy visions mock the spirit's seeing.

Fading in the blue ether, now 'tis passed
   Beyond the bounds of sight, and left us yearning
To follow after; for it seems at last
   But to its own bright home above returning.

And yet 'twas but a little time ago
   When all that seemed but now such joy and grace.
Bound down to earth was held, a vulgar show
   For gaping crowds in yonder market-place.

Fiercely it struggled then, but all in vain: [ing
   Too strong the cords that checked its upward tend-
Till, freed by some kind hand, from this dull plain
   Proudly it rose, to kindred worlds ascending.

So now the spirit frets against the ties
   That bind its pinions down to earthly things.
So gladly would it seek its native skies,
   Might Opportunity but loose its wings.

Unsatisfied.

Tell us, ye wise, why is it that in reading
   Of what the world's great men have said or known,
Their thoughts, our own to contemplation leading,
   Remind us still of what may yet be done?

Why is it, when with Milton's Satan hovering
   Between his first bright life and endless doom,
The soul can never rest, nor cease discovering
   New realms of light or deeper depths of gloom ?

Why is it that, in Byron's wild creations
   Unsatisfied, though thrilling with delight,
We pause not even at his outer stations,
   But still pursue the far, etherial flight ?

Why, over Moore's luxurious Eastern story,
   Filled yet not satiate with its gorgeous bloom,
Picture we still new worlds of golden glory,
   Where richer flowers more balmy gales perfume ?

Why, even when most earnestly admiring
   All that is great and beautiful and true,
Must we be still unsatisfied, aspiring
   From what is done to what man yet may do ?

Tell us, ye wise, is not this constant yearning
   For something better, this desire to rise,
But Nature's promise of the soul's returning
   To brighter realms beyond our mortal skies?

Yes, they are true, those words of sacred story:
   The Perfect One on earth to save us died.
Through Him the soul regains its pristine glory;
   In Him at last we shall be satisfied.

To My Soldier Brother.

We are thinking of you to-night, brother,
    We are thinking of you to-night.
As we gather here at home, brother,
    By the hearth-fire's cheerful light.
Our mother looks round the circle,
    And the tear-drop dims her eye;
And we ask her not the reason,
    For our own hearts tell us why.

We speak not, for our thoughts, brother,
    Are busy with the past—
That sad yet happy time, brother,
    When you were with us last.
And then, in solemn sadness,
    Our father kneels to pray;
And each heart repeats the earnest plea
    For the dear one far away.

We are thinking of you to-night. brother,
    And not to-night alone;
For often a thought of you, brother,
    Is hid by a careless tone;
And oft in the midst of pleasure.
    Or as toil returns again,
Will a look of pain o'ercloud the brow—
    We are thinking of you then.

If the prayers of those at home, brother,
    Can smoothe the soldier's life,
Or a loving faith avail, brother,
    In the terrible hour of strife,
The assurance still be yours, brother,
    Wherever you may roam,
Or whate'er the time, while life shall last.
    We are thinking of you at home.

What Shall I Wish You?

What shall I wish you—beauty, wealth or fame?
    For many a woman's heart has sighed for these,
Though beauty fades, and fame is but a name,
    And wealth too often drives away all ease—
    And you have now enough of each to please—
Or a light, gentle spirit? Or a mind
    Solid, yet womanly, and quick to seize
Each subtile meaning? Or a taste refined?
These would I wish, and more, had you not all combined.

Yet will I wish—and though the thoughtless heart
    May lightly jest of life's most sacred ties,
And deem me acting but the trifler's part,
    Your judgment is too seriously wise
    Not to perceive how much the wish implies
Of all the purest, deepest joys of life,
    Of peace on earth, and even in Paradise
Of added bliss beyond all care and strife—
May he who wins your hand be worthy such a wife!

————()————

My Vision.

The night was dark; the autumn winds were sighing
    In fitful gusts, and scattering drops of rain,
From the low clouds that southward fast were flying,
    Pattered upon the roof; and I, in pain
    And weakness, lay and listened, while each vein
Throbbed with a boding sense of coming ill;
    And something I could feel but ne'er explain—
A strange, mysterious awe—o'ercame my will.   [chill.
And hushed my fluttering heart, and made my blood run

The very air seemed full of unseen evil;
    And I could fancy, 'mid the gathering gloom,
Each deeper shade was but a lurking devil
    On dread design intent. Some awful doom
    Seemed just impending. Were the demons come
Up from their torments to prepare new woes
    For guilty man? How soon, alas! should some,
Unthinking now, ere even this night should close,
Deep anguish feel, or seek their long, their last repose!

I slept at last, worn out by anxious fears—
    But sudden seemed to waken, with a scream
Of piercing horror ringing in my ears;
    And calling me, too, did its accents seem.
    Then, with the quick transition of a dream,
A late-deserted battle-field I trod,
    In search of *him*, while the moon's pitying gleam
Cast sickly radiance on the blood-stained sod   [God.
Where thousands, unprepared, had gone to meet their

At last, 'neath a low willow's drooping shade
    I found him, my dear, only brother lying
In a dark pool his own life-blood had made.
    Wildly I called him: "Brother, are you dying?"
    No answer but the low, convulsive sighing
And gasp for breath. Oh God!—And then I tried
    To rouse him; and at last he too seemed trying;
And then his strange, wild eyes were opened wide,
And his stained hand pressed hard upon his bleeding side.

But ere he died he knew me, grasped my hand,
    And murmured "Brother!" faintly, sweetly smiled,
And looked toward Heaven. And in that better land
    I hope to meet him, and am reconciled
    To sorrow here. Say not my vision wild
Was but a feverish dream; for soon there came
    News of a "glorious victory"—so 'twas styled;
But I read only my dead brother's name.
    Yet later years with grief shall mingle pride;
    My brother nobly for his country died.

Call Me Not "Friend."

Call me not "friend;" I will not be thy friend.
   Mine must be names that have a deeper meaning;
For by thy promise, till thy life shall end,
   Love's is the harvest, Friendship's but the gleaning.
Give to thy friends all Friendship calls its own,
But give me only, love, thyself, thyself alone.

Call me not "friend;" it is a sacred name;
   But I am more than any friend to thee.
To each true friend give all a friend may claim,
   But thou thyself shalt wholly cleave to me.
Mine is the feast; when Love is satisfied
Let Friendship come; but thou thyself art mine, my bride.

————0————

The Dearest Spot.

The dearest spot on earth to me
   Is where my loved one dwells;
And still to it my fancy turns,
   For still my love impels.

There is no other home for me,
   No other spot so fair
As that where lives my darling, for
   My heart is with her there.

I love the place where she has been,
   And more than all the rest,
The spot where first I called her mine
   And pressed her to my breast;

But ah! their living charm is gone;
   And still the feeling swells,
The dearest spot on earth to me
   Is where my loved one dwells.

When shall I greet her eyes' bright glance,
   Her voice's gentle tone,
And feel her dear lips press the kiss
   Of welcome on my own?

When shall I find that happier place
   Than all the world beside,
Where home for me is blest by her,
   My dearest one, my bride!

———()———

The Volunteer's Song.

Brothers, the country is calling, is calling:
   Now is the moment of peril and fear.
Haste to the field where our brothers are falling!
   Quick, to the rescue! Why linger we here?

Join us, all ye that have courage and spirit!
   Join us, all ye that can shoulder a gun!
Loud sounds the war-cry; say, do ye not hear it?
   On to the field! Let our duty be done!

Now, brothers, ready! May God grant His blessing!
   Sisters, pray for us; be hopeful and true.
All that on earth would be worth your possessing
   We must defend now. God bless you! Adieu!

Brothers, we come. Stand ye firm; falter never.
   Fast to your aid rush we on to the fight.
Forward! The flag of our country forever!
   On to the battle, and God speed the right!

With a Locket Picture.

Joy now, thou poor, faint semblance of myself,
For thou shalt rest secure, and dearly cherished
With eloquent looks and kisses, where even I
Not now may dare aspire; and mayest thou be
An ægis to my loved one! Would to Heaven
Thou might'st have power to ward off every ill !
And as thou hold'st sweet converse with her heart,
Tell thou my love, even there upon its throne;
And all my life shall make thy promise good.

Oh, were I but as thou, the toils and sorrows
That rise before me now, were then no more;
No struggling with the world, no race for fame,
No ceaseless, weary toil for daily bread,
No longings for the future, then should try me.
Thoughtlessly happy, on that bosom ever
Would I recline, and this one happiness
Should be the world for me. But now, alas!
What weary days and restless nights shall come
While time and distance part my love and me !

Oh, were I but as thou—but no; I would not;
For there will come a time when manly love
And faith and hope shall have their full reward,
When I shall clasp her to my heart, my bride;
And that one hour, with its quick, passionate joy,
Shall more than balance all life's cares and troubles.
Heaven speed the day, and then the calmer bliss
Of wedded life prolong in happy years!

———()———

I Know that Thou art Faithful, Love.

I know that thou art faithful, love;
    But oh! this constant pain
Of absence from thee! Dearest love,
    When shall we meet again?

I hope each day is happy, love,
    In thy far home, for thee;
And I would never pain thee, love,
    By one sad thought of me.

But oh! my soul is weary, love,
    Of this so long delay,
And longing for the coming, love,
    Of that thrice-happy day

When smiling fate shall witness, love,
    The sacred service done
That joins our lives forever, love.
    As now our hearts are one.

Yet will I trust the future, love,
    Though dark the present seems;
For still beyond the clouds, dear love,
    The steady starlight gleams.

I know that thou art faithful, love;
    And this the charm shall be
To cheer my fainting spirit, love,
    While I must wait for thee.

——()——

The Coming of the Springtime.

I am longing for the springtime
    With its bright and happy hours,
When the sunshine laugheth merrily
    To greet the opening flowers,
And the gentle breezes fanning us
    With softly rustling wings
Stop to listen to the mocking-bird
    In careless glee that sings.

Now the dark and dreary winter
    Deepens round the cheerless camp,
While the chilled and weary sentry
    Breasts the night-winds cold and damp;
And our hearts grow faint within us
    As the story comes once more
Of our brothers slain by thousands
    On the far Potomac's shore.

But we trust the God of Nations,
    That ere many days be past
He will bring these times of evil
    To the hoped-for end at last;
And the coming of the springtime,
    With its budding trees and flowers,
Shall behold a glorious peace in all
    This happy land of ours.

I am longing, ever longing,
    Dearest, for that happy day;
And the thought of it sustains me
    As the long months wear away;
For with peace to all 'twill bring to me
    A dearer blessing far,
When thy love shall be my crown of joy,
    As now my guiding star.

Oh, the coming of the springtime
   Shall be beautifully bright,
As the morning comes in glory
   After all the gloom of night.
Then, when man with earth rejoices
   In its newly-wakened life,
Shall our long, dark night of trial
   Have its morn of joy, my wife.

———o———

Linda, My Darling.

Linda, my darling, long have I wandered;
   Many and far have my travels been.
Now to the dear old valley I'm coming,
   Weary and worn returning home again.
Linda, my darling! Linda, my darling!
   Echoing o'er the lake the sounds are flying.
   Ah, if her own dear voice replying
Sound but the hunter's joyous welcome home!

Often together here we have lingered;
   Oft o'er the lake she has answered my song.
Once more the winds from the kind old mountains
   Waft the old tones of love and hope along.
Linda, my darling! Linda, my darling!
   Is it an echo, or the breezes sighing?
   Ah! 'tis her own dear voice replying
Joyous in welcome back to her and home.

———o———

The Lost Love.

You kindly inquire of the grief I conceal;
    You would offer some solace of pain;
But my sorrow is one that this earth cannot heal,
    For the dead return never again.

Ah, how bright were the days of that blest long ago
    When my love and my life were in bloom!
But how gloomy and dark is this long night of woe
    Since my loved one was laid in the tomb!

I have wandered for years, till I knew not a home;
    I have tried every means to forget,
But in vain; for thoughts of the Past will come,
    And the lost love haunts me yet.

But the time will come, it may be soon,
    And I only wait till then,
When the trials and woes of earth are done,
    And loved ones shall meet again.

————0————

The Angel of the Storm.

Once, out on the gentle summer sea
I took my little boy with me.

Only the waves' long roll was there;
And the sky was clear, and the wind was fair.

No helping hand would I take along;
For I knew the ways of the sea, and was strong.

And oft in that little boat before
I had joyed 'mid the tumbling billows' roar.

So lightly now I sailed out to sea
Alone, but my little boy with me.

Soon I noticed the breeze was growing strong,
And was glad, for it sped our boat along,

Till now from the land, if we could be seen,
We showed but a speck on the ocean's green.

And my boy laughed out, as we ran with the wind,
"Oh, Pa, what a wake we leave behind!"

But a cloud arose, as the wind grew high,
And fast it spread o'er the darkening sky.

So, rather from prudence than any fear,
I turned, for a landward course to steer.

But the storm grew fast; the wind was a gale;
And I felt my power on the tiller fail.

Then I moaned, as one in sudden pain,
And crouched 'neath the whirling drifts of rain.

And, poorly sheltered beside my knee,
My dear little boy spoke wistfully:

"Oh, Pa, I am wet and cold. Now, come;
We have sailed enough: let us hurry home!"

"My child," I thought—though I said not thus—
"These billows are earth's last home for us."

And then, with a sudden awe, not fear.
I felt a Spirit presence near.

He spake: "Our Father rules the storm.
"If He wills it so, you are safe from harm."

He passed. My soul was cheered though awed,
And strong with an Angel's trust in God.

Ere long, through the cloud-banks far in the west
Came a sunset gleam, and the storm had ceased.

Some Power had guided us through the gloom;
For we saw the land, and were near our home.

Three Miles to Camp.

Onward marching, ever onward
　　Through the forest lone and drear,
Now fatigue almost o'ercomes us;
　　Scarce our limbs their burden bear.
Still the evening shadows deepen,
　　But no sign of rest appears
Till a horseman comes to meet us,
　　And his glad shout greets our ears:

"Three miles to camp;　Three miles to camp!"

Now with strength renewed, our footsteps
　　Measure off the weary way,
Till before us "Rest and supper"
　　Camp-fires brightly shining say.
Stretched at ease, we now remember
　　How the day dragged slowly by,
And how quickly changed our feelings
　　When we heard that cheering cry.

So, though gloomy all around us
　　Now the war-clouds seem to lower,
Peace may not be very distant:
　　This may be the darkest hour.
If a message from the future
　　Could but like that horseman come
It might cheer us now with promise
　　Soon of greeting Peace and Home.

———o———

Going Home.

Thank God! We're going home!
No more the deep-mouthed cannon's vengeful roar
Or the fierce musket's rattling roll shall come—
No more, no more!

No more the warning cry
"Halt! Who comes there?"—the watchful, straining gaze,
Shall warm the chilling blood with danger nigh,
In coming days.

No more the dull routine
Of camp, its wearying drills and toilsome show—
Muster, parade, review—affect us now:
These all have been.

No more on scorching sand
Or through the gloomy swamp our course we lay,
Where lurks an enemy on every hand,
By night or day.

No more the dreadful scene
Of battle-field or hospital shall come
The happy dreams of future days between:
There's peace at home.

War's awful night is past.
Oh, who can tell the heart-felt happiness
Of this dear morn of Peace that now at last
Has come to bless!

———()———

Wake, Wake, the Song!

Wake, wake the song, a song, a song of gladness.
  Loud let us raise our cheerful notes of joy.
Yes, now bid adieu, adieu to care and sadness;
  Banish every thought that pleasure might alloy.
      While the gladsome sounds are ringing
          And the choral strain
          Re-echoes once again,
      Since there's no better voice for joy than singing,
      Why should my tuneful heart from song refrain?

Welcome to all who love the voice of singing!
  Oft as the year shall run its course again
May scenes like this return, still with them bringing
  Pleasures ever dear to all who gather then.
      And when life for us is ended,
          May the songs of earth
          Have new and higher birth,
      And with the joyful notes of angels blended
      Help to sound the endless hallelujahs forth.

———o———

Welcome Song.

Welcome, welcome to our circle,
  All whom song has gathered here,
As with lightsome, joyous music
  Greet we now the glad New Year.
      (Chorus.)   Welcome, welcome, etc.

Far away be care and sorrow;
  Joy shall rule the hour to-night;
Then sweet dreams; and on the morrow
  Song shall make the day more bright.
      (Chorus.)   Welcome, welcome, etc.

And when all life's joys and sorrows
   Shall for us be passed away,
As we "gather at the river"
   May we hear the angels say,
       (Chorus.) Welcome, welcome, etc.

———O———

Rosalie.

Yon little valley's narrow bound,
Where the huge rocks stand like guardians round,
Is dearer than all the world to me,
   For there lives Rosalie.
Through the valley a brooklet free
Ripples in ceaseless melody;
Always happy it seems to be,
   Singing for Rosalie.

Fair are the flowers in that valley low;
For lovelier all things there do grow;
But fairer than all the flowers is she,
   My darling Rosalie.
For her their richest colors bloom;
For her they all the vale perfume.
And oh, how happy they must be,
   So near my Rosalie!

The sun shines there with a softer light,
And the moon with a tenderer radiance bright,
For down in the valley there they see
   My darling Rosalie.
And the brightest of all the stars that spread
Their glittering splendors overhead
A special guardian seems to be
   For darling Rosalie.

Down in the valley all day long
The wild birds sing their sweetest song—
But what were the voice of the birds to me,
    Without my Rosalie?
Thoughts of her their sweet notes bring:
Still to me they seem to sing,
"Oh, how happy, happy are we,
    With darling Rosalie!"

Soon the happiest day shall come;
There in the valley I'll make my home;
And the joy and light of my life shall be
    My darling Rosalie.
All the sky is bright for me;
Brighter still it soon shall be.
Oh, the bliss of a life with thee,
    My darling Rosalie!

————O————

Yankee Doodle's Centennial.

When Yankee Doodle came to town,
    A hundred years ago, sir,
Full heavy was he weighted down
    With care and want and woe, sir.

'Mid rudest scenes, on roughest fare,
    He passed his early life, sir,
While lamentations filled the air
    Through eight long years of strife, sir.

But faithfully he struggled on,
    For Independence fighting,
Till Victory upon him shone,
    With Peace and Hope uniting.

And then for seventy years and more
  He grew and prospered greatly,
Enlarged his borders and his store,
  And came to look quite stately.

His flag of stars throughout the world
  In pride and glory floated,
Though on its stripes, where'er unfurled,
  Still one dark stain was noted.

But since with blood and many tears
  He washed the stain away, sir,
The best of all his hundred years
  We celebrate to-day, sir.

In all the land each breeze that swells
  That flag now floating o'er us
Bears boom of cannon, peal of bells,
  And music's joyful chorus.

For Yankee Doodle greets the day
  More glad than e'er before, sir;
And fervently we hope he may
  See many a hundred more, sir.

————()————

Bostonese.

High o'er the Ecmyrean mount
  Where huge Euphrastos plumes his wings,
While by the pure Castilian fount
  Cephalia softly sips and sings,

There on his huge agetic seat
  Great Atropos his treasure spreads,
And heeds no more the storms that beat
  In doubled thunders o'er our heads.

O Atropos, majestic Name!
  One boon I crave, one blessing seek:
One spark of that celestial flame
  That animates our modern Greek.

I kneel, I bow. I know not whence
  The highest intellections flow;
But though there may not be a Hence,
  The present Thisness I would know.

He heard, and from his torch of light
  One lambent ray responsive shook,
Which, darting through the nether bright,
  A hitherward direction took.

And on my brow its radiant glow,
  Absorbed, resistant, reigns sublime.
I thrill with ecstasy; I know
  The Thisness of recursive time.

O joy superm! O extant bliss!
  O ye who understand the These
And know the Otherness of This,
  I'm one of you: I'm Bostonese!

———()———

In Miss E---'s Album.

As Friendship joins with Love and Art
  To make this book a treasure
Where care and sadness have no part,
So may life's tracings on your heart
  Be only those of pleasure.

A Retrospect.

Ah, Mary, when we both were young,
    A quarter-century ago,
What walks we took, what songs were sung,
    What blissful hours we used to know!

Yet I would not bring back again
    Those hours, though sweet their memory be:
Too far the changing years since then
    Have separated you and me.

We dwell not far apart; we see
    Such meetings as by chance occur;
But other lives would different be,
    Had ours been what I thought they were.

Though in that first sweet dream of love,
    Those halcyon days of youthful bliss,
The joy all other joys above
    I valued was my Mary's kiss,

Since then, I own, I've found in life
    Some rather more substantial joys:
For I've a happy, loving wife.
    And half-a-dozen girls and boys.

The blossom of our youthful life,
    To fruit more solid later grows;
And truly as I love my wife,
    You love your husband, I suppose.

So when we meet no look is seen,
    No word is said, a thought to show
Of what we were, or might have been,
    A quarter-century ago.

The past is dead, and we grow old;
    The gray is mingling in our hair;
Yet still my heart your form shall hold,
    My Mary, ever young and fair.

Changed.

We talk about the weather,
  My lady fair and I,
And idly wonder whether
  The day will be wet or dry.

A year ago, a meeting
  Like this was bliss for me;
And the kiss she gave in greeting
  Was a thrill of ecstasy.

I loved her, oh, so madly!
  And it almost broke my heart
When she told me, oh, so sadly,
  That we for a year must part.

She sailed across the ocean
  For a European tour;
And my letters breathed devotion
  For which words seemed all too poor.

She returned with new airs and graces,
  And with manners far more free;
But though still as fair her face is,
  She is not the same to me.

So we talk about the weather,
  And—paradox of the heart—
The more we are together,
  The farther we are apart.

———o———

Quid Pro Quo.

MRS. J.—I think, my dear, we'll have to give
    A party once or twice this season.
You know, we cannot always live
    Just for ourselves; and there's no reason
Why we, who go so much, should be—
    MR. J.—We never go unless invited.
SHE—I know, my dear; but don't you see,
    We may some time be badly slighted
Unless we give——HE—O yes, I know—
Unless we give the *quid pro quo.*
  { HE—It's always so; it's always so;
  { SHE—You're quite correct; it's always so;
BOTH—We mustn't forget the *quid pro quo.*

HE—Well, then, of course we'll have to make
    Some inexpensive preparation;
For instance, say ice-cream and cake.
    SHE—Why. Charles! think what a reputation
We'd get if, after all we've been
    Where lunch was served in style so splendid,
Our own should be so cheap and thin:
    Our social life would soon be ended.
HE—I guess you're right; in fact, I know
It would not be the *quid pro quo.*
  { SHE—You're quite correct; it's always so;
  { HE—It's always so; it's always so;
BOTH—We mustn't forget the *quid pro quo.*

HE—Well, have it as you wish, my dear;
    I'll leave to you the preparations.
SHE—All right; and as the time is near
    When we must send the invitations,
Let's make a start. HE—Well, Elsie Gray:
    You know, she plays and sings so sweetly.
SHE—Oh yes; that's what you used to say

When you adored her so completely,
But two or three short years ago.
Is she what you call *quid pro quo?*

HE—Oh dear! no, no; oh dear! no, no;
SHE—I'd like to know, I'd like to know
HE—She's nothing like a *quid pro quo.*
SHE—Just what you mean by *quid pro quo.*

SHE—Now, I would start with Charlie True.
 HE—The cad! Wears paper cuffs and collars!
SHE—Well, General Brown. HE—'Twould never do:
 I owe him fifteen hundred dollars,
And he might think——SHE—Indeed he might.
 How easy some such escapade is!
So let's agree that you invite
 The gentlemen, and I the ladies;
And then, you see, each one will know
How best to give the *quid pro quo.*
BOTH—That's just the thing, for each will know
How best to give the *quid pro quo.*

BOTH—And so it's settled now, we'll give
 A party once or twice this season.
Of course we cannot always live
 Just for ourselves; and there's good reason
Why we, who go so much, should be
 To meet our friends at home delighted,
Since now we've taken care to see
 That none has cause for feeling slighted.
I think, my dear, we've fixed it so
That each shall have the *quid pro quo.*
It should be so; it shall be so;
We'll never forget the *quid pro quo.*

———o———

Anniversary.

Dear wife, when, thirty years ago,
    In promised love we clasped the hand,
We did not think and could not know
    How long a time that promise spanned,
How Fate should part us soon and far,
    And sickness add its pains and fears,
And how the awful storm of war
    With danger fill the lengthened years

Of separation; then and there
    We only knew we two were one,
And humbly asked God's loving care
    For all the new life thus begun.
And in the years of wedded life,
    In every change of good or ill,
You've been a true and faithful wife,
    And I have tried my part to fill,

Just as we promised; and perhaps,
    Though when life's records we retrace
We see full many a name in caps
    And ours in common lower-case;
Though hopes have been full oft denied,
    And all ambitions overthrown,
And Fortune's favors turned aside,
    And sorrows many we have known,

It may be, if we could but know
    What might have been, what may be yet.
We'd own that all is better so,
    And gladness would efface regret.
At any rate, still fond and true,
    We'll humbly try to do our best
For us, and ours, and others too,
    And trust the Lord for all the rest.

JOSEPH.

A PARAPHRASE.

SCENE 1—*Jacob's house. Jacob discovered, alone. Enter all his sons except Joseph.*

Judah. Grace to thee, father, and full length of days!
Jacob. My blessing on you all! But where is Joseph,
The son of my old age?
Reuben.   We know not, father.
He was not with us last night, or indeed
The night before. He's seldom with us now.
I don't know where he is.   [*Enter Joseph.*
Joseph.   Grace to thee, father!
And you, my brothers, a good day to you!
Jacob. A father's blessing on thy head, my son!
But wherefore stayest thou not with the rest?
They say they have not seen thee for two days.
Joseph. Indeed, they have been out to feed their flocks,
And I have lingered here at home the while.
And oh! I had the strangest dream last night!
I dreamed that while we all were binding sheaves,
I bound one, and behold! it rose and stood
Upright upon the ground, and all your sheaves
Bowed down to mine, to do it reverence.
I never had so strange a dream before.   [dream!
Simeon. Well, now, that must have been a pleasant
Thou hast our father's love more than we all;
But shall we really all bow down to thee
And do thee reverence? No, thou idle boy;
Thy foolish dream shall never come to pass.

Dream on, for thou hast nothing else to do.
But, brothers, we must go unto the fields,
And watch our father's flocks with all our care,
While Joseph lingers here at home to dream.

[Exeunt all but Jacob and Joseph.

Jacob.   Joseph, my son, 'twas but an idle dream.
Thou should'st have kept it to thyself; thy brother
Did scorn thy telling it. Come to me, Joseph.
Thou art my latest-born, my flower of age.
I love my children all, but unto thee
My soul doth cleave with love more cherishing.
Wear thou this robe in token of that love.

[Gives Joseph a colored robe.

Yet when thy brothers meet thee, do not boast,
Or tell them more than that I gave it thee.

Joseph.   I thank thee, father; and I do believe
I love thee more than all my brothers do.
I will not go with them to-day. I think
They've little love for me, I know not why.
I'll stay at home to-day, as Simeon said.
They do not want me to go out with them.

Jacob.   God's love be with thee, Joseph, even as mine!
Then, if thou hast His love, no brother's hate,
If that should come, nor even the wild beast's fangs,
Nor aught that's harmful, e'er can hurt thee, Joseph.
Yea, though thy foes should cast thee in a pit.
Or seek thy life, God would deliver thee.
And turn their evil to thy greatest good.
Ill cannot come to him whom God doth love.

Joseph.   I thank thee, father, for thy holy words.
I'll ponder them.

Jacob.   May God watch over thee! [Exeunt.

————o————

SCENE 2—*Jacob's house. Jacob and Joseph together. Enter
the other sons.*

Jacob.   Well, my good sons, how fare ye with the flocks?
Levi.   Well, father; but in truth we watch them not
As closely as we have sometimes before,
Because we muse upon our brother's dream.

Joseph. Now, good my brothers, be not angry with me.
I did but tell a dream. And lo! last night
I dreamed another one; but that I'll keep,
Nor wound you more with telling of a dream. [dream?

    Dan. Come, tell! [*Aside.*] Why can I never have a
Or if I have, why must it have no meaning,
No pleasant one, like his?—Come, now; thy dream!

    Joseph. Well, be not angry with me then, my brothers;
For it was but a dream—[*Aside.*] Yet two such dreams!—
An idle dream, just like the other one.
I dreamed that I was in the field again,
But now alone, and that those self-same sheaves
Did as they did before, and then the sun
And moon stood out together in the heavens
And made obeisance. 'Twas a foolish dream.

    Jacob. A foolish dream—but was it all a dream?
I have had dreams that were not dreams alone;
For God sometimes in them, to me, His servant,
Hath gracious shown His future workings forth.
But what shall two such dreams to thee portend?
Shall we, thy father, mother, and thy brothers,
All bow to thee, and make obeisance to thee,
The youngest of the flock? Shalt thou rule over us?
Go to! 'Twas but a dream. Yet I have dreamed.
But doth God manifest His will to thee,
To thee, my son, my youngest son, my Joseph?
Come thou with me. Thou should'st not tell such dreams.
Yet I will keep them in my heart, and see
What fate the Lord may have in store for thee.

                [*Exeunt Jacob and Joseph.*

    Dan. O. what a dainty dreamer is the boy!
This is because our father gave the robe
Of many colors to him. Yesterday
His dream meant only we should bow to him;
But now the robe so works upon his mind
That father, mother, all, must kiss the dust
Before his lordship. Oh, I see him now
Sitting in state, while we, his elder brothers,
Poor shepherds as we are, with shame and fear

Do come before this favorite of his father
And, prostrate in the dust, with bated breath,
Do beg our lives of him, and call ourselves
His bounden servants if he so may grant.
Oh, he's a dreamer!

 Judah.   Thou dost chide him, Dan.
For that wherein there is no blame to him.
He did but tell a dream, at our demand—
An idle dream born of his idle thoughts,
Such as we all have. What is wrong in that?
I've often dreamed as idle dreams as this,
And told them, and we thought no more of them.

 Simeon. No; but no one of us has dreamed such dreams
As this of Joseph's, and with such a meaning.
It shows his thoughts, as plain as words can be.
We know our father loves him more than us;
What if he should make over all his store
To him, and so set him up over us?
We are but shepherds; we must tend the flocks;
And he, the youngest, may inherit all.
But, brothers, if you will but help me now.
I have a plan to get him out o' the way. [*Enter Jacob.*

 Jacob. Why, Levi, Simeon, Dan, why frown ye so?
Why go ye not betimes unto your flocks?

 Levi. We did but marvel why it is that Joseph
Should always stay at home here and do nothing.
He's old enough to help us.

 Jacob.   Go to now!
I told him he should stay at home to-day.
Where feed ye now?

 Reuben.   In the vale of Shechem, father;
And 'tis so far, we come not back to-night.

 Jacob. Why, then, to-morrow I will send out Joseph,
And ye shall send me word again by him
How fare ye all. But treat him well, I charge ye,
When he shall come. Now go ye with my blessing.
              [*Exit.*

 Simeon. Aye, so we will. We'll show him how to dream,
And how to tell his dreams. Come, we must go.
              [*Exeunt.*

SCENE 3—*A plain. Joseph's brethren tending sheep.*

Judah. But, Dan, what reason have we so to slay him?
How has he injured us, except in these
His idle dreams? 'Tis true, our father loves him
More than us all; but this is not the way
To win our father's love—to slay our brother.
I have no cause to love him, more than thou:
But still, a brother's blood's a heavy sin.

Dan. The sin upon my head! I fear it not.
Besides, we do not slay him: we but cast
Him in the pit; and then, if 'tis to be
That we must serve him yet, as he has dreamed,
Why, then so be it: we can't hinder it.

Judah. Well, I am sworn. But be it as thou sayest:
The sin upon thy head. [*Aside.*] Yet were it not
That I am sworn, I'd ne'er agree to it.

Dan. Stand to it all, then. He is coming now.
I'll speak to him; the rest keep still, but bind him,
Nor let his words or looks undo your purpose.
Make haste and hide, and at the word spring on him.

[*All hide except Dan. Enter Joseph.*

Joseph. Hail to thee, brother! What! Art thou alone?
For I have brought ye greeting from our father,
And his good blessing.

Dan. Why, how now, thou dreamer!

[*All the concealed brothers, except Judah, rush out, seize Joseph, tear off his colored robe, and drag him, with tumult, across the stage, Dan following. Exeunt omnes. Enter Judah alone.*

Judah. The deed is done; and I am sworn to silence.
Down, thoughts! I did not have a hand in it.
I will not think of it. I did not do it.

[*Murmur of persons approaching from both sides of stage. Enter from one side all the other brethren except Joseph, and from the opposite side several Midianite merchants.*

1st Midianite. Well met, shepherds! Greeting to you!
We spied you as we passed, and came to see if we could
buy or sell with you to-day. We go now down again to

Egypt, and would rather buy. But it's like we cannot. Shepherds buy nothing, for lack of money, and sell nothing because they have nothing to sell. By my beard, were I a shepherd, then should I never bother my poor brains to buy and sell and get gain. What then would it be to me that the market is now down in Egypt, or how then should the quarrels of two kings affect my purse? Verily, war should not trouble me: war meddleth not with sheep. Egypt might change kings, the world might rise and fall, and I should know it not. What would I have to do with wars, or kings, or nations, or markets, arts, sciences, or sins or virtues? My king, priest, nation, art, science. everything, should be sheep. If I would be strong. that should be big sheep: if I would be wise. that should be many sheep; if I would be wealthy, that should be more sheep. Virtuous I would be, as sheep are virtuous, sinning not, for knowing not how to sin. For what should I murder, but sheep? Or how should I lie, to my sheep? Verily, in my dreams I would cry Baa! Oh, if a man would only live, let him be a shepherd. If he would have fame, so; if he would have wealth, so; if he would be wise, so: but why should a man be famous, or rich. or wise? Yea, why

[Enter 2d Midianite.

should he live? But if he would only live, let him tend sheep.——What saidst thou. Elikim? Bought a man? Bought a man from these shepherds? Brother? These gentle shepherds sold us their own brother? O ye good shepherds, innocent shepherds! Twenty pieces? Why, there's a bargain there—but if he's like them, they've got the bargain.

2d Midianite. We have indeed bought their brother; and he looks a goodly youth. They hate him because of some strange dream about his father's colored robe, or something of that kind; and they have but just now cast him in the pit over there at the edge of the wood. I went and saw him, poor fellow!—but they will not go near him again, lest he move them by his words. And now, if thou art in the humor, thou mayest give these

good shepherds thy parting blessing; and then we will
pass by the pit, weigh out our purchase, and so go on to
Egypt with good hope of gain.

1st Midianite. Well, so be it. And now, shepherds, innocent shepherds, even as he is innocent whom ye fear
and worship and call the devil—I do eat all my words.
May all your lord's and master's richest blessings rest
upon ye! But if I had to be either of you, I would take
my chances in your brother's place instead of yours,

[*Exeunt Midianites.*

Dan. Oh, if that Midianite had been alone,
I would have stopped his railing. But now, brothers,
The day is waning; we must home to-night.
But how shall we account unto our father
For Joseph's absence? Nay, I have it how:
We'll kill a kid, and in the blood of it
We'll dip the robe, that lies here on the ground,
And give the pretty rag another color,
And say to-night, we found it, and we think
A lion must have met him on the way
Before he reached us. Would not this be best?

Levi. The very thing! Come, let us hold to that.
But I will kill the kid: I love to do it;
I do delight to see the blood spirt out
Its bright red stream; and then the little kid
Turns up its pretty eyes so mournfully,
I love to see it. Come; I'll kill the kid. [*Exeunt.*

———o———

SCENE 4—*Jacob's house. Jacob and family discovered; he
holding the colored robe.*

Jacob. It is his robe; it is my Joseph's robe;
The evil beast hath torn my son in pieces.
God's will be done! But oh, my son, my Joseph!
My heart's delight, the flower of my old age!
My joy, my comfort! Have I lost thee, Joseph?
Must I hear nevermore thy gentle voice
Calling me father? Oh, my son, my Joseph,
Would I might have laid down my life for thee!
I would have yielded up my withered years

With joy, could I but see thy face, my Joseph.
Thy voice would soothe my passage to the tomb
Even as an angel's whisper. But, Oh God!
Now I must tread the wilderness of life
Unto the dreary end, and long for death,
And when it comes drop glad into my grave.
Oh, it is terrible. The pangs of dying
Are ten-fold multiplied by youth and strength:
But to be torn by piecemeal, limb from limb,
To meet the hungry lion's rage alone,
With none to help or hear—Oh, it is terrible.
Oh God, in mercy let me also die!

Adah. Weep not so sorely, father. Hast thou not
Thine other sons remaining? And with Joseph
Is perfect peace and joy in Paradise.
We do but selfishly deplore our loss,
Which is the greatest gain for him we mourn.
Let us now comfort thee. Thine other sons,
Who always have their ready service done,
Shall put new duty on, and be more tender
In care for thee, and so shall we, thy daughters.
Our common loss shall give us better love,
And we shall knit us closer to each other,
And grow more fond with mutual suffering.
Our Joseph's memory shall be our mentor
When we would stray from right; and so our life
The better for our grief shall pass away,
And we shall then meet Joseph, and his voice
Shall be our first, glad welcome after death.
Oh, 'tis a bitter, bitter grief, my father,
But God shall sanctify it to our peace.
Even so, His will be done!

Reuben.   I too, my father,
Would comfort thee, but that my burdened soul
Can find no words meet for its utterance;
And I should prove but a poor comforter.
Father, I can but share this grief with thee.

Judah. Our father, wilt thou not be comforted?
Lo, we thy sons, even as our sister Adah

Hath said, will be more dutiful to thee.
We do confess we have not done enough
To cheer thy waning years; but we shall all
Do better service with more reverence now,
Our only care to cheer thy stricken heart
And charm away thy grief by showing us
So gentle and so dutiful that thou
Shalt come to feel thy loss is recompensed
In our more love; so let us comfort thee.

Jacob. My sons, I thank ye for your kindly words,
And thee, my daughter; but have ye the power
To banish grief with promise of a future?
Ye have a brother's, not a father's, heart;
And youth is strong, and promises itself
A quick forgetfulness of all its sorrows;
But age shuts out all thoughts of consolation,
And mourns a loss as if 'twere loss of all.
No, I cannot, will not be comforted.
Ye say my Joseph's dead; ye come and tell me
My youngest son is eaten by a lion;
And then ye say, Be comforted! I will not.
He was your brother only, but to me
He was my son, my youngest son, my Joseph.
Comfort me not: I'll not be comforted.
For forty days and nights I'll sit and weep,
In sackcloth and in ashes, for my son.
And yet, that dream! Oh, God of Abraham
And of my father Isaac, give me faith,
That I may know Thy mercy even when
Thy ways are most mysterious! Thou didst bid
An angel stay the hand that would have slain
My father Isaac, on the altar bound,
Obedient to Thy word. Oh, grant me faith
Beyond all doubt, that even in this woe
Still I may know Thou doest all things well.

     [*Solemn music, while curtain slowly falls.*

———0———

CHORUS.

Days have passed; and now behold
Joseph into bondage sold.
But all along the toilsome way
The wondering Midianites would say
His God was with him, for he seemed
Sure in faith of what he dreamed,
And he showed no sign of hate
Of his brothers or his fate,
Though to such a depth descended,
Instead of what that dream portended.
Who now, of all the gay and brave,
Would bow to this young Hebrew slave?
But there is a Power above
Can change oppression into love,
And from the common market-place
Can take the slave of foreign race
And give him e'en a prince's grace.
Who then of us should now despair?
The God who worked such wonders there
Is just the same to-day as then,
And loveth all the sons of men.

The slave to Egypt's market brought,
By wealthy Potiphar is bought,
Upon whose mind the Lord has wrought
In Joseph's favor. He has heard
The Midianites' mysterious word
That God was with him. They have told
Of haps and chances manifold,
When Joseph's presence seemed to cheer
Their hearts and drive away all fear.
And Potiphar, impelled by Heaven
For greater ends, to him has given
The care of all his goods and lands,
And at the head of all he stands.

Some little time has passed away;
And Joseph's favor day by day
Has grown apace, till now he's seen
Of manly frame and gentle mien,

As one that's born a court to grace
With noble form and faultless face.
No more a simple shepherd youth,
Nor yet a common slave, forsooth,
Though still in bondage, he is now
One to whom other slaves must bow;
But though so strange his fate has been,
His heart is pure and true as then.

———o———

SCENE 5—*Potiphar's house; his wife discovered, alone.*

Zillah. Must this be so? Must this young Hebrew slave,
Whom Potiphar bought from the common market
And hath so made the ruler of his house—
Must he still scorn me? Is it not enough
He is my equal, aye, and even more,
In Potiphar's esteem and confidence?
And shall he scorn me, whom he should obey,
When I do offer him myself for love?
Even Pharaoh himself might ask in vain
What I do offer to this Hebrew slave,
For love of him—and he refuses me.
I have tried all my arts to compass him;
I have enticed him with alluring looks,
And spoken sweetest words into his ear,
Of secrecy and love; and in his sleep
I've fondled him and kissed him till he woke
And turned away from me. Yet I am young
And fair. Why doth he hold himself so high?
Am I not good enough? He's but a slave—
And yet indeed he is no common slave,
With such a history. I pity him;
Yea, more, I love him, who should be his mistress
But cannot be, though he doth still obey
In everything but this, where he should be
Most willing. Yet I own he bears him well.
He hath more influence with Potiphar
Than I myself; and even I do love him,
Who should be jealous of him, and from whom
He is too proud to take the highest favor.

But I will either win or humble him.
Even now he comes—I know that manly tread.
I'll make one last attempt, and if I fail,
Love turned to hate shall have its quick revenge.
                    [*Enter Joseph, as if to pass by.*
  Joseph. Good morrow to thee, my most gentle mistress!
  Zillah. Good-morrow, slave! Stay; I would speak with
There's none in sight or hearing; Potiphar   [thee.
Is gone from home; here's opportunity;
Come, dearest, come; I die of love for thee.
        [*She seizes Joseph's robe, but he flees, leaving it behind.*

Refused and scorned; scorned by a common slave!
Now for revenge! I'll show him what it is
To scorn a woman. Isis, aid me now!
Help! Help! [*Enter Zakel and other servants*]
                    Ha! Zakel, seest thou this robe?
It is that Joseph's robe, that Hebrew slave's,
Whom Potiphar hath so raised over you.
He came—but he has fled, and left this robe.
Hence! Seek and bind him till your lord comes home.
And, Zakel, straightway summon Potiphar,
From me, to come at once, but say not why.
                    [*Exeunt servants.*
    So now, proud Joseph, I will glut myself
With sweet revenge at least, since love is lost.
I'll show thee now, thou upstart Hebrew slave.
That thou art yet a slave, and I thy mistress,
And that I yet have power with Potiphar
Which thou hast not usurped. I'll put thee now
In proper place. I've shown thee how a woman
May cheapen down herself to nothingness
For love, and now I'll show thee what a treasure
A woman's favor is, that thou hast scorned.
                    [*Enter Potiphar.*
  Potiphar. Hail, gentle mistress; Wherefore didst thou
  Zillah. Knowest thou this robe?   [call?
  Potiphar.   Why, yes; 'tis Joseph's robe.
I gave it to him but the other day,
For some good deed, I don't remember what,

Among his many nameless ones.   What of it?

Zillah.   It is his robe; and wearing it, he came
Into this room while I was here alone
Studying some new delight for Potiphar,
And tried—Oh, Potiphar!—But I cried out
With all my voice, and at the sound he fled;
But as he went I plucked the robe from him,
To show thee, oh, most noble Potiphar.

Potiphar. What? Has the slave whom I have favored so
Dared to attempt my honor? By the gods!
For this ingratitude he shall rot out
His base, unworthy life in Pharaoh's prison.   [slave
Ho, Zakel ! [*Enter Zakel.*] Straightway find that Hebrew
Called Joseph; bind him well, and bring him hither.

                          [*Exit Zakel.*

The slave! This, when I have so favored him,
And made him ruler over all my house,
And given all my store into his hands!
The Hebrew slave! Zillah, 'tis well for thee
Thou didst prevent him; else this scimetar
Had slain ye both. I cannot slay him now:
There is not cause under the law of Egypt;
But he shall lie in prison all his life,
And wish for death. Zillah, now get thee hence,
And purify thyself from Joseph's touch.

Zillah.   Most noble Potiphar—
[*Enter Zakel and other servants, bringing Joseph, bound.*
Potiphar.   Thou Hebrew slave!—
But I am Potiphar: I will not speak
To thee.

Joseph. My noble lord——

Potiphar.   Hence with him straight
To Pharaoh's deepest dungeon, there to stay
Till I shall order otherwise. No words!

        [*Exeunt Zakel and other servants, with Joseph.*

Zillah (*aside.*) Oh, sweet revenge!   [*Exit Zillah.*

Potiphar.   Oh, base Ingratitude,
This is thy worst! The slave whom I had made
The ruler over all my house, and loved
Even as a son, repays my kindness thus!

Oh, he is worse than an ungrateful son,
For I have been more than a father to him.
Children are bound to us by natural ties,
And care for them is care but for our own:
But he was naught to me—a common slave,
Of a strange race—and yet I gave him all
I could have given a son—and all for this!
Oh, base ingratitude! And yet in truth
Until this day he never gave me cause
For any doubt, but always showed himself
Worthy still higher trust, as more he gained.
With prudence always he has watched my store,
And with sound wisdom often counseled me.
Until I thought he was the best of men;
But now this damnable ingratitude
Has blackened him forever in my mind.
Now will I nevermore trust any man:
Joseph was false. Oh, base ingratitude!   [*Exit.*

——o——

CHORUS.

Falsehood triumphs; bound and gagged,
Joseph's now to prison dragged.
This the fate of manly beauty:
This the fate of pious duty;
Now in the dungeon's deepest ward,
From every joy or comfort barred,
Behold him there who ruled so late
A prince's house. Oh, cruel fate!
        But God is with him, now as ever.
And soon he wins the keeper's favor.
And sarce a month has waxed and waned
Till he such change of state has gained
That all within the prison's done
On his authority alone.
And all but freedom is his own.
Yet he is but a prisoner still;
And to a prisoner's bounded will
E'en pleasures are but sad; the free
Alone have joy, with liberty.

SCENE 6—*A hall of the prison.*

Baker. But why should we, who have both been here now for some time together, both have such strange dreams in the same night? And why should we both dream of threes? I do believe the gods have thus darkly shown us what shall be our fate; but we have here none of the magicians.

Butler. Then must we be our own interpreters; and therefore do I tell thee thy dream meaneth that thou must be hanged.

Baker. In good mercy now, butler, do not prophesy evil unto me, for here have we all enough. But is there any among ye, fellow-prisoners, who can interpret dreams?

1st Prisoner. Thou knowest Joseph, the Hebrew, who now ruleth here in the prison. I think, if any here can show the true meaning of a dream, it must be he, for there is a saying that his God is with him. And indeed I know not how else he could have so won favor with the keeper, who is a very Memnon without the music.

Butler. Why, yes; I know Joseph, for I have seen him often with the keeper, and when he makes the round of the prison. It must be about the time for a round now; and he may be here soon. We will tell him our dreams; and if his God is with him he can tell us the meanings.

[Enter Joseph.

Joseph. Good-morrow to you, fellow-prisoners!
But wherefore looks our baker so to-day—
Even as a man who should be hanged to-morrow?
Art thou not ill, or hast thou heard bad news?
Can I do anything to help thee, friend?

Butler. My lord Joseph, thou art the very man of whom we were speaking as thou didst open the door. This it is with the baker, and with me also, though it troubles me not as it does him: we have dreamed strange dreams, and there is none to interpret them; but my friend here said that if there were any in this prison who could tell the meanings, it must be my lord Joseph.

Joseph. Interpretations do belong to God,

Not man; but tell thy dream, my friend, I pray,
And God may give interpretation to me.

Butler. Well, this is my dream; and may thy God
give thee a happy meaning. I dreamed last night that,
there was before me a vine having three branches, and
even while I looked the vine budded and blossomed, and
brought forth ripe grapes in clusters. And Pharaoh's
cup was in my hand; and I took the grapes and pressed
them into the cup, and gave the cup into Pharoah's
hand. This is my dream.

Joseph. The interpretation of thy dream is this:
The vine's three branches signify three days;
And in three days shall Pharaoh lift thee up
From out this prison, and restore thy place;
And thou shalt give his cup into his hand
As butler, even as in former days.
But think of me when it is well with thee—
That I am still a prisoner, as thou wast--
And speak of me, I pray, to Pharaoh.
That, by thy favor, I may leave this dungeon.
For I indeed was stolen away from home,
And made a slave; and I have done no wrong
For which I should be cast into this prison.

Butler. Here's a health to thee, my lord Joseph, if I
did but have the wine; and when I dream again thou
shalt interpret for me, for thou hast indeed a gift. And
now for our friend the baker. Canst thou not cheer
him up also? He is very sad to-day.   [wills

Joseph. Tell me thy dream, my friend; and if God
I'll show its true intent. What didst thou dream?

Baker. Thou didst give the butler a happy meaning;
and if thou wilt but do the same for me I will be thy
bounden servant when it cometh to pass; for indeed I
am sore troubled in mind, fearing that evil is about to
come upon me. But this is my dream which I had last
night in my cell, even as the butler had his; and may
thy God give good of it to thee and me: I dreamed that
on my head were three baskets full of holes, one basket upon another; and in the uppermost basket were
all manner of baked meats for Pharaoh; and evil

birds came and ate the meats from the baskets upon my head.

Joseph. My friend, I can but show thee as it is.
It is not I who do interpret it,
But God; therefore be thou not angry with me,
For I do pity thee. This is thy dream:
The baskets on thy head are yet three days;
And in three days shall Pharaoh lift thee up
And hang thee on a tree; and evil birds,
Vultures and crows, shall eat thy flesh from thee.
This is thy doom. May God have mercy on thee!

Baker. Go to, now! Thou art a false prophet. I will not believe thee. Thou and the butler have conspired to jest with me; and I like it not. Put not on so grave faces. Ye saw that my dream troubled me, and now ye seek to vex me further. But I'll leave ye to your own good spirits. Just now joking suits not with my humor; so I'll go back to my cell. Good-morrow to you. [*Exit.*

Joseph. Oh man unfortunate! Would I might save!
Yet God hath so ordained. But I do tarry
Too long. Good-morrow, fellow-prisoners.

All. Good-morrow. May thy God still be with thee!
[*Grouping, as Joseph retires, and curtain falls.*

———o———

CHORUS.

Thus Hope's feeble ray has come
To Joseph in the prison's gloom.
So doth sunshine cheer the heart
When heavy clouds a moment part.
But still deeper cold Despair
Folds her gloomy mantle where
Hope hath pierced it, and doth cover
The buried ray more deeply over.

Now a hope doth Joseph cherish--
Doomed, alas! to quickly perish—
That, free once more, the butler will
Keep his prison memory still.

Longing yet patient doth he wait;
But disappointment is his fate.
Dreams, not bars, he can unfold:
Wisdom hath not power like gold.
   Two full years have passed away.
Hope died long since, day by day.
Still that stern, relentless door
Casts its gloomy shadow o'er
The prisoner; still within its bound.
Dreary duties' changeless round.
Where now, Joseph, is thy dream?
Did it such a fate foreseem?
'Shall this prison be thy grave?
Dream'st thou now, Egyptian slave?
Dreams have sold thee: can they save?
Shall thy God no more show favor?
Shall He now no more deliver?
Yes. Despair, in vain thy spell:
Faith shall triumph; all is well!

——o——

SCENE 7—*The palace. Pharaoh on his throne; nobles and attendants around; priests and magicians in their robes, and with incense and implements of magic apparently just used.*

  Pharaoh. O wise magicians! Have I called ye forth
From all our Egypt thus to no avail?
Can ye not tell the meaning of a dream?
Where is your magic? Summon all your powers;
Try all your arts; call every spirit up
That ever did or may obey your bidding.
Cannot our sacred priests expound a dream?
Call on the gods. Ye never prayed before
For such a cause as this that calls ye now:
For unto us, or haply to our Egypt,
I know my dreams do shadow some strange ill,
Which I would fain avert. Call on the gods.
Am I not Pharaoh? I do command ye
That ye do find the meaning of my dreams.

By all the powers of earth or sea or air
I do adjure ye. Nay, I'll give to him
The half my kingdom, who doth tell my dreams.

1st Magician. Most mighty lord, most noble Pharaoh,
We cast us in the dust beneath thy feet,
Our lives are at thy word; but all our wisdom,
And all our prayers and arts, and all our magic,
Are powerless to expound great Pharaoh's dream.

Butler. I do remember me my fault this day,
Most noble Pharaoh. When thou wast angry'
With me, thy servant, and I was in prison
With Hez, the baker, we had each a dream
In the same night; and when we cast about
To find a man who could interpret dreams,
There was then in the prison a young Hebrew
Named Joseph, whom the keeper much did favor.
To him we told our dreams, and he explained
Their meanings; and the future came to pass
Just as he said; and there was in the prison
A saying that his God was with him and—

Pharaoh. Cut short thy prating; go and seek this Joseph
With all thy speed; and when thou findest him [means,
Bring him straight hither. [*Exit Butler.*] I will try all
Since all your arts and prayers avail me naught,
To find the interpretation of my dreams;
For I do fear they have the same intent,
And that of evil. But have ye not left
Some deeper charm? Leave nothing in your power
Untried; and half my kingdom will I give
Him who succeeds

1st Priest. Most noble Pharaoh.
Rinos Pilesar, the last Priest of Memnon,
Posessed one spell more powerful than all others;
And ere he died, with the most scrupulous care
In Memnon's sacred statue he concealed it,
And bade me, his successor, use it not
But on the utmost need; and yesterday,
As I was bowed before the holy statue,
The parchment issued thence and came to me
Of its own power. I have it here with me;

But on such hard conditions is it based
That he that useth it doth straightway lose
All former powers, and thenceforth for three days
Doth languish, and then die; and being used
By any other than a Priest of Memnon,
Or if another man doth see its use,
It then doth lose all further potency.
But at most noble Pharaoh's command
I'll use the spell, though it shall cost my life.

[*He makes preparations, and burns incense. The stage
grows dark, and then is lighted with red fire. Weird music is
heard at a distance. Various strange shapes appear, as if of
summoned spirits. The Priest chants the spell:*]

      Armath beroson, am polusophi!
      Al Ierosoman, ho, Arobar!

[*Lightning and thunder. The strange music becomes
louder, as if approaching. There is an appearance of a man's
head in fire. It vanishes with a terrible crash; and the stage
instantly assumes its former appearance.*]

  Pharaoh. Why, this indeed was still more terrible
Than all the rest; but did it tell my dreams?
Speak! Tell me quick!
  1st Priest.   Most noble Pharaoh!
There is no power in all the world of spirits
That mortal man may call at thy command,
That can expound the meaning of thy dreams.
Some mightier Power, unknown, above them all.
Above us all, above all other powers,
Doth overrule them now. When I go hence,
In three days more, let my line cease with me.
Memnon was great.   [*Enter Butler, with Joseph.*
  Butler.   Most noble Pharaoh,
This is the Hebrew slave of whom I spake.
(*To Joseph.*) Bow down to Pharaoh.
  Joseph.   I bow myself.
What would he with me?
  Pharaoh.   Listen now, young Hebrew.
I, Pharaoh, now sitting on my throne,
Last night did dream, but not a common dream,

For it holds evident some import deep
Of hidden ill to me or to my throne;
And being troubled much this morning by it,
I called the Priests, the Wise Men and Magicians,
Who have tried all their prayers and all their powers,
And there they stand, and cannot tell my dream.
But it is said of thee that thou canst show
The meaning of a dream: therefore I brought thee
From out the prison; and if thou dost tell
The meaning of my dream I'll give to thee
Half of my kingdom.

   Joseph.   It is not in me:
Interpretations do belong to God.
But, if it please thee, tell thy dream, my lord,
And God shall give thee its interpretation.

   Pharaoh. I in my dream upon the banks of Nile
Was standing; and there came up from the river   .
Seven well-fleshed kine, and fed them in a meadow;
And after them came up seven other kine,
Lean-fleshed and poor, such as I never saw
In all the land for badness; and these last
Did eat up the first seven well-favored kine,
And then remained as lean-fleshed as before.
Then I awoke, but fell asleep again
At once, and straightway dreamed a second time;
And in my dream, behold! seven ears of corn
All rank and good, sprang up upon one stalk;
And after them, behold! seven other ears,
All thin and blasted by the east wind, sprang up;
And these last seven devoured the seven good ears,
And then appeared no better than before.
Now, canst thou show me the interpretation?

   Joseph. Thy dreams are one, my lord; and God doth
To Pharaoh what He will surely do.   [show
The seven good kine and seven good ears of corn
Are seven good years that shall come now in Egypt;
And the seven lean-fleshed kine and blasted ears
Are years of famine that shall follow them.
And as the years of plenty shall be such

As Egypt never knew, so shall the famine
Be such as shall blot out their memory.
And God vouchsafed the dream to Pharaoh
A second time because He has ordained it
And it shall shortly come to pass.　Now therefore
Let Pharaoh select a man of wisdom
And set him over all the land of Egypt,
That he may gather up the surplus grain,
Even the fifth part of all that shall be raised
In the seven plenteous years, and store it up
In granaries; and let prudent overseers
Attend to this in every place, and urge
The people to lay up yet other store
Against the famine, for it shall be sore
In all the land.　God hath so spoken it.

　　Pharaoh.　Now, verily this is the true intent;
It doth comport most fully with my dream.

　　　1st Priest.　It is indeed the true interpretation.

　　　1st Magician.　The Hebrew doth exel us all in wisdom.

　　　Butler.　His God is with him still, O Pharaoh.

　　　Pharaoh.　Now, where shall such another man be found,
One whom his God doth favor and give wisdom?
Now, therefore, Joseph, since thy God hath given thee
More wisdom than is else in all our Egypt,
I will do better for thee than I promised
Him who should tell my dream: thou shalt be ruler
O'er all my house and all the land of Egypt,
And only in the throne shall I be greater,
And by thy word shall all the land be ruled.　　[on him,
[*To attendants.*]　Take ye my robe and chain, and put them
And lead him here, and seat him by my side. [*They do so.*]
Now mark ye all!　This is our royal pleasure:
Do ye by him as he were Pharaoh.
Sound, heralds: Hail, and bow the knee to Joseph!

　　　Heralds.　Hail! Bow the knee! Hail! Bow the knee to
　　　　　　　　　　　　　　　　　　　　[Joseph!

　　　All. [*Bowing the knee.*]　Hail to thee, noble Joseph! Hail,
　　　　　　　　　　　　　　　　　　　　[all hail!

　　　　　　　[*Curtain falls, to triumphal music.*]

CHORUS.

Dreaming Hebrew youth, and sold
By brothers' hands for strangers' gold;
Sold into the Egyptian's hands—
Ruler over all his lands;
Now, falsely blamed, in prison thrown—
Now Egypt's all but king alone;
Now, thy grace and wisdom proved,
Be Egypt's pride, by Egypt loved.
Nevermore in trouble be:
God shall ever prosper thee.
Wisdom and grace to thee are given,
Peace on earth, and bliss in Heaven.
Now is fulfilled thy youthful dream:
O'er a great realm thou art supreme.
But shall thy brethren to thee bow?
Yes, and thy grace their lives allow;
But other duties claim thee now.

Abundant waves the golden grain
While smiling Plenty holds her reign.
The surplus of the fruitful years
In heaped-up granaries appears.
Now Egypt rings with joy and pride
When Joseph weds a royal bride.
And Potiphar has mourned his fate,
In better knowledge, all too late;
But Joseph's love is still more great
Than was his own, and, while he lives,
To Potiphar due favor gives.

The seven years pass; and now, behold!
The famine comes, that was foretold.
In vain the farmer guides the plow:
No harvest sheaves shall cheer him now.
But Egypt gives the wisdom praise
That warned her of the coming days,
For now were all her people dead
If Joseph's granaries had not bread.
Not here alone is famine found,
But dearth in all the country round;

And as it spreads, still spread the more
Reports of Egypt's ample store,
Until men come from every land
To buy them food at Joseph's hand;
And strangely thus, as God hath willed,
Is Joseph's dream at last fulfilled.

———o———

SCENE 8—*A court of the palace. The butler, Joseph's steward and a number of officers, conversing.*

1st Officer. Now, steward, tell us how it is about those
Hebrews for whom my lord doth make so much trouble
—he who always doeth only good to all others. There
is something very strange about the matter; and thou
knowest more about it than we do, so tell us about it,
we pray thee.

Steward. I do believe these Hebrews must be some
whom my lord knew before he came into Egypt. and
that he has some motive which I know not, else why
he should so vex them I cannot understand. But this is
what I do know of the matter; and the butler also
knows a portion of it: About the time when men first
came here to buy corn, these Hebrews came, among
others, before my lord. And when he saw them, he
spoke roughly to them, so that we who knew him won-
dered. "Ye are come as spies," he said, "to discover
the nakedness of the land." And they answered that
they were not spies but true men, all the sons of one
father, and that they had left their younger brother
behind them when they came. Then my lord grew
strangely angry; and he bound them, and kept them
for three days, and then had them brought before him
again, and told them that they must go and bring their
younger brother, and that he should keep one of them
bound here for surety. All he said to them was through
an interpreter, too; but I noticed that when they talked
together among themselves, my lord changed color, and
then he went out for a few minutes; and when he returned he caused one of them to be bound before their

eyes. Then he commanded me to fill their sacks with corn, and to put back each man's money in his sack; and so I did, and sent them away unknowing.

Butler. What! So long ago? There is certainly something strange about this matter. My lord Joseph must have some secret motive; for he is to all men kind and merciful, even as he was with poor Lord Potiphar and his wife, as you all remember.

2d Officer. Why, yes; I remember that it made great talk at the time; and I knew something of the matter, but not all. Wert thou not concerned in it in some way?

Butler. Why, no, not more than indirectly; but I knew all the facts at the time.

2d Officer. Tell us, then. It may throw some light on this last subject.

Butler. I doubt it. But it is a strange story. It was while I was in the prison that my lord Joseph came there, consigned by Lord Potiphar, who would not hear any defense from him. But after the king had brought my lord Joseph to the court to interpret his dream, and my lord had found favor in his eyes, then did the king question him as to his history; and when my lord told him how he had been sent to the prison, then did the king send for Lord Potiphar and his wife and brought them before him when Joseph was not present. Now my lady Zillah dared not lie to the king, but confessed the truth. Then the king summoned my lord Joseph and commanded him to give judgment; and my lord forgave Lord Potiphar for his unjust haste, and remembered only his kindness. Moreover my lord said he could not find it in his heart to punish the lady Zillah; but indeed he had no need, for hardly had she seen him when she sank into a swoon and was borne away; and though she lived for two days she was never conscious again. You must all have heard of this, for it was known to all the court.

2d Officer. Yes, I knew of a part of it; and I remember that while poor Lord Potiphar lived, my Lord Joseph heaped kindness on him. But tell us, steward, knowest thou nothing further of this matter of the Hebrews?

Steward. Yes indeed do I; for now the Hebrews have come again; and this time they brought balm and spices and other presents for my lord, and double money for that which was put back in their sacks; and they brought us also their younger brother, and came and stood before my lord. And when he saw them in the audience room, he bade me make ready for the Hebrews to dine with him to-day. But they seemed to be in much trouble; and they came to me with an interpreter, and told me how they had found the money in their sacks, and had brought it back; and I calmed them, and brought out to them their brother whom my lord had kept here as surety. And at the hour I brought them before my lord, with their younger brother and their presents; and they bowed themselves before my lord, and offered their presents through an interpreter. And through him also my lord inquired of them about their welfare, and about their father, and spoke kindly to their younger brother whom they had brought with them as he had commanded. And then he seemed greatly excited in some way, but tried to hide his feelings, but could not, and went out from the room. But he soon came in again, and caused a table to be set for them, and another for him by himself—for it is an abomination to eat with a Hebrew.

Butler. I was there then, and waited upon my lord. And he caused the Hebrews to be seated according to their ages, and sent portions from his own table to them; and to the youngest of them he sent five times as much as to any of the rest. And they ate and drank and grew merry, so that I thought they never before had drank so good wine or so freely.

Steward. And afterward my lord commanded me again, and again I filled their sacks with corn, and put their money back into their sacks; and this time, as he commanded me, I took my lord's silver cup from his table and put it in the mouth of the younger brother's

sack of corn, and sent them all away again, but a little
while ago. And this is all I know of the matter. [*Enter
a messenger to the steward.*] But my lord sends for me,
and I must go now. I'll warrant there is more to do
with those Hebrews. [*Exit Steward.*

1st Officer. Well, my lord may vex them now, but it
must be for their good, I'd lay my life on it.

[*Curtain falls.*]

———o———

SCENE 9—*Joseph's house. Enter Joseph and the steward,
meeting,*

[brews?
Joseph. Well, steward, how now is it with the He-
[lord.
Steward. Why, even as thou didst seem to wish, my
I found them at short distance from the city,
And charged upon them as thou didst command;
And then they all turned pale with sudden fear,
And all declared they knew not of the matter,
But said that if the cup were found with them,
Then should he die who had it, and the rest
Would be thy servants. At their word I took them,
And straightway made them open each his sack,
And searched them all, from eldest down to youngest,
And found the cup where thou didst bid me place it.
Then they all rent their clothes in grief and fear,
And straightway loaded every man his beast,
And came back with me, as thou didst command.
Even now they wait without.
Joseph. Good! Bring them hither.
[*Exit steward.*]
Oh, my dear brothers! Give me strength, O God,
For yet a little further needful trial.
My soul yearns for them, though they sold me once,
And mocked my dreams; and I must show them now
That Thou didst thus foreshow what was to be,
And was and is and shall be. Thou art true,
And they shall bow, even as it was foretold;

And then—but now they come.
[*Enter steward, with Joseph's brethren, who bow before him.*

   Steward.   My lord, the Hebrews.

   Joseph.   What have ye done now, Hebrews? Knew ye
That I can speak your language? Knew ye not   [not
That such a man as I can make a trial?
Am I not ruler here? And did ye think
That ye could steal my cup from off my table,
And then escape my wrath? What, knew ye not
That I could tell even your most secret sins,
Even to the vilest deed of all your lives?
What say ye now?

   Simeon.   My lord, what can we say?
How can we speak? How shall we clear ourselves?
God hath found out thy servants' wickedness;
And now not only he who had the cup
But all the rest of us shall be thy servants,
If it shall please thee thus to spare our lives.

   Joseph.   No; I will be more merciful to you:
But he who had the cup shall be my servant,
And all the rest may go again in peace
Unto your father.

   Judah.   O most gracious lord,
I pray thee let thy servant speak a word.
My lord enquired of us, thy servants, saying
Have ye a father, or another brother?
Then answered we my lord: We have a father,
And one more brother, son of his old age,
Left only of his mother. He is dead
Who was his brother; and his father loves him.
Then did my lord command thy servants, saying,
Bring here your brother, that I may behold him.
Then said we to my lord, It cannot be:
His father loves him; and if he should leave him,
Then would he die of grief. And my lord said,
Except your younger brother come with you,
Ye see my face no more. And when we came
Up to thy servants' father, then we told him
Thy words, my lord, and all that had befallen.

And when the corn was gone, our father said,
Go down again and buy us further food.
And we said, We may not go down again,
Except our brother Benjamin go with us;
For thus the Governor did strictly speak.
Then said our father unto us, Ye know
I had two sons; and one of them is not;
And now if ye do take the other from me,
Ye bring me down with sorrow to the grave.
Now when thy servants come unto our father
Without our brother, since our father's life
Is bound up in the lad, then will he die,
And so thy servants shall bring down our father,
In his old age, with sorrow to the grave.
And then thy servant made himself a surety
Unto our father for our younger brother,
Saying, If I bring him not again with me,
Then shall I bear the blame to thee forever.
And now I pray thee let me be thy bondsman,
And let the lad return unto his father.
For how shall I go up unto our father
Without the lad, and see my father's sorrow?
I pray thee let me stead thee for the lad,
For I became his surety.
      [*Joseph motions out all the Egyptians.*

 Joseph.   Oh, my brothers,
My brothers! I am Joseph, whom ye sold.
My brothers, Oh, my brothers! Be not grieved
Or angry with yourselves that ye did sell me;
For God hath sent me for a great deliverance.
Be not afraid: I am your brother Joseph.
Fear not. There shall no evil come upon you.
'Twas God who sent me hither, at your hands,
To save your lives: for now two years the famine
Hath been, and there shall come yet five years more;
And God hath made me ruler of all Egypt,
That I might lay up food against this famine.
Now therefore ye shall go up to our father,
And bring him hither, him and all his house,
And ye shall all dwell in the land of Goshen.

And I will feed ye; for in all this Egypt
Ye know that I am even as Pharaoh.
And I will stablish ye and all your house
In Goshen; ye shall tell our father so.
Do ye not hear me? Am I not not your brother?
Are ye not glad to see me yet alive,   [my brother,
As one raised from the dead? [*To Benjamin.*] And thou,
My mother's son; our father loved us both
When we were with him; now, in other years,
He'll love us yet again, restored to him.
Forgive me, brothers, if I served ye hardly:
'Twas but to make a trial of your truth,
I do forgive you for the wrong ye did me.
Let us be brothers once again together.

> [*Joseph embraces Benjamin, and the curtain falls.*]

——o——

SCENE 10 —*The grand audience hall of the royal palace.
Pharaoh discovered, seated on the throne and surrounded
by a vast assembly of lords, nobles and people.*

[Joseph?

Pharaoh. The time has come; why comes not our good
1st Officer. Most noble Pharaoh, he went to meet
His father and his brothers, who have come,
At Pharaoh's command, to dwell in Egypt;
And even now they enter at the court.

Pharoah. I knew he would be here: he never fails.
I thank the gods that sent me such a friend,
Discreet above all others, tried and true.
While he is with us, Egypt will be safe. [*Enter 2d Officer.*

2d Officer. Most noble Pharaoh, I bear a message
From my lord Joseph, saying that he comes,
And asking that he may not be announced,
But enter with his father and his brothers,
Whom he would now present to Pharaoh.

Pharaoh. Whatever Joseph wishes shall be done.

Give orders now that no salute be made
To him until I give the signal for it.

[Enter Joseph, supporting his father, and followed by his brothers. All salute Pharaoh.]

Joseph. Most noble Pharaoh, at thy command
I bring my father and all these my brothers,
To do thee honor, and to dwell in Egypt.

Pharoah. Thou doest well—thou doest all things well.
I bid them welcome here; and for thy sake
The best of Egypt shall be given them.
But as for thee, come thou unto thy place;
For I indeed am Pharaoh, but thou
Art ruler. Come. Sound, heralds, Hail to Joseph.

[Grand flourish of trumpets.
. [Joseph!

Heralds. Hail! Bow the knee! Hail! Bow the knee to
All. Hail to thee, noble Joseph! Hail, all hail!

[All bow, including Jacob and his sons; and triumphal music sounds, while Joseph advances to the foot of the throne.]

Joseph. Most noble Pharaoh——
Pharaoh. Most noble Joseph,
Take thou thy place; and bring thy father up,
And seat him and thy brothers by thee here.
All Egypt is before thee: settle them
Wherever thou shalt choose; and they shall dwell
In peace forever. Be it thus recorded.

[Joseph ascends to seat at right of throne, and sends ushers who bring his father and brothers and seat them near him.]

Joseph. My lords and nobles, I salute ye all.
Ye heard most noble Pharaoh's command.
This is my father and these are my brothers;
And in the land of Goshen they shall dwell
In peace; and when yet five more famine years
Are passed, prosperity shall come again,
And they and all our Egypt shall be happy.
My lords, ye know the story of my life,
And how for this deliverance I was brought
To Egypt; and in this my hour of joy

Because my father and my brothers all
Are with me, ye will surely join with me
In welcome and rejoicing; and in token
Of gladness, let there be an order sent
Throughout all Egypt that there shall be given
From our storehouses unto all who need,
One day's provision, and so on this day
In each year of the five of famine coming.
So shall our people all have cause for joy.
And on this day shall everywhere be told
The story of the dream of Pharaoh,
And how God gave him its interpretation,
And Egypt thus was saved.

   Pharoah.   So shall it be.

[*Joseph salutes Pharaoh, who gives a signal, whereupon the assembly rises, with joyful acclamation; music sounds; and the curtain slowly falls.*]

POTOMAC SERIES, NUMBER 1.

Potomac Series is the name of a little quarterly issued by the Woman's National Press Association, in which Mrs. H. B. Sperry, a member of the Washington society, has an interesting but peculiar story of open vision.—New Church Messenger.

* * *Containing several readable articles by various authors. "Invisible Intervention," by Mrs. Sperry, is a strange story, founded upon facts, relating to the life of one of the noble men who pioneered the way for others in the early settlement of Ashtabula County, Ohio.—Church Watchman.*

Potomac Series, No. 1, is a tastily-gotten-up little volume, the first of a series of short sketches, and if its successors come up to the standard established by the first volume the series will be a valuable addition to the list of such publications. The little book is full of interesting reading from the initial letter to the scroll that closes the last page.—Washington News.

*The first volume of Potomac Series contains two sketches by Mrs. E. S. Cromwell, an accomplished woman; a West Indian romance by Miss Foster; one of East India by Mrs. Hort; and Mrs. Sperry gives a touch of the uncanny; to say nothing of the other sketches. * *As a collection of Short Stories, this first issue compares favorably with the fiction of most of the magazines.—New York Commercial Advertiser.*

*Potomac Series, No. 1, is the title of a new periodical published in Washington. It is neat and attractive in style.. * *Contains seven short sketches, each being full of interest and very different in character. Pen pictures, drawn from life, depict scenes in different parts of the United States and in the East and West Indies. * *The little volume is well worthy of notice, and as the Potomac Series is the first short story periodical ever published in this city we trust it may meet with encouragement.—Washington Post.*

Potomac Series for July contains a true story of a most remarkable experience of the father of the writer, Mrs. H. B. Sperry, of the Woman's National Press Association of Washington, D. C. Injured near unto death by the falling of a limb from a tree in the forest, he is led across fields, with hand clasping in the air the hand of an invisible friend, to friends near home, who then take him to his wife, who has been unusually anxious during his absence that day concerning him. As soon as he was able to speak to his friends in the road, though there was a horrible cut in his head, and he was covered with blood, he declared himself perfectly happy in the company of friends in the spiritual world, from whom he was reluctant to part except for his wife and child.—The New Christianity.

POTOMAC SERIES, NUMBER 2.
SPERRY STORIES.

Arthur Sperry, a Washington newspaper boy, has embodied his experiences as a police reporter in a small volume. These stories are interesting, and show that their author is a very clever writer, and thoroughly at home in depicting scenes which came under his own personal observation in the modern Babylon. The book is published simultaneously in Washington and London. Mr. Sperry is at present vice-consul of the United States at Swansea, Wales.—*Evening News*, Washington, D. C.

Washington newspaperdom of five years ago knew Arthur Sperry as one of its own; to-day the one-time reporter has a reputation on both sides of the Atlantic as a writer of short stories. Some of his efforts are remarkable for their excellence—especially those that deal with the Chinaman as he is in a great American city. In more than one of the popular English magazines there is always a place for a contribution from Mr. Sperry, sure evidence of real merit, for the Briton is not enthusiastic without good cause over American products of either the material or literary varieties.--*Washington Star*.

Sperry Stories is a collection of twelve short stories (some of which are quite thrilling) by Arthur Sperry, son of the founder of the News, and published in neat booklet form as No 2., Potomac Series.—*Ashtabula* (Ohio) *News*.

Mr. Arthur Sperry. nephew of the Hon. E. F. Sperry of Knoxville, and an employe in the consul's office at Swansea, Wales, has written a collection of short Chinese stories, the scenes laid in the Chinese portion of New York. Young Sperry was born in Iowa, and Hawkeye brains in this instance are up to a high standard of literary excellence.—*Iowa State Register*.

We have just had the pleasure of perusing twelve entertaining stories contained in book form, and written by Mr. Arthur Sperry. of the American Consulate, Swansea: and we venture to think that the work, at the price of the nimble shilling. will find a ready sale. "Qaong T.n." "Hop

Wah, Philosopher,'' and two or three other stories display an intimate knowledge of the habits of the Chinese in America that could only be obtained by personal relations and close observation. Whilst anything relating to Japan or China is intensely interesting just now, perhaps the special charm of "Sperry Stories" to the local public is the fact that the plot of one of the prettiest of the tales, '' Meg and Ben,'' is located at Gower.—*Cambria Leader*, Swansea, Great Britain.

Certainly, Mr. Sperry, of the United States Consulate at Swansea, possesses all the essentials of a pleasing story-writer. The book recently published by Messrs. Gay & Bird, 5 Chandos street, Strand, London, consists of a dozen smartly-written tales. Mr. Sperry is particularly happy in those efforts which deal with Chinese life in America. "Quong Tin" and "The Hatchet Society for Fin Tien" are real literary gems, scintillating with the spirit of the century's end. "Saved by a Sphygmogram," and "Hop Wah, Philosopher," are also admirably penned. Anything appertaining to Chinese manners or methods is of interest at the present moment, and Mr. Sperry's revelations are as curious, sometimes even weird, as they are interesting. Distinctly American in tone and treatment are the sketches entitled, " A Failure," " R. A. T. S,'' " A Woman Who Did Not," and "Cox's Blunder.'' The author's command of the dramatic element is well shown in "Said the Paretic,'' '' The Inspector's Cat." and "The Jade Snake.'' There is considerable charm in Mr. Sperry's style. It is very terse and picturesque, the thoughts being just sufficiently daring to keep the reader on the constant *qui vive*. We must confess to a feeling of dissatisfaction with the only local story included in the book. "Meg and Ben" is located at Pwllddu, and probably the author inserted the legend by way of compliment to the *locale* of his present sojourn. On this ground is it only excusable. The tale has neither pith nor plot; it even lacks the lightness and vivacity of the writer's other contributions. But as against this lot of paste, the rest of the book may be compared to a string of pearls. Eminently readable, we do not hesitate to advise our readers to purchase a copy and peruse Mr. Sperry's creations for themselves.—*Swansea Gazette*.

This number sent post-paid for 25 cents, by
H. B. SPERRY, 321 Delaware Ave. N. E.,
Washington. D. C.

POTOMAC SERIES, NUMBER 3.

HOLIDAY NUMBER—JANUARY, 1895.

—·.·—

POTOMAC SERIES, NO. 3. has Poems and Stories by a number of well-known writers, among whom are

Mrs. E. S. Cromwell,
Mrs. L. A. Crandell,
Mrs. F. C. Dieudonne,
Mrs. Sylvie Sperry Eberhardt,
Mrs. May Whitney Emerson,
Miss Mary F. Foster,
Mrs. Rosetta L. Gilchrist,
Mrs. Emily F. Hort,
Mrs. M. D. Lincoln,
Mrs. Mary S. Lockwood,
·Mrs. Evarts Ewing Munn,
Mrs. Mary M. North,
Miss Lilian Pike,
Mrs. H. B. Sperry,
Miss M. E. Torrence,
Mrs. Dora T. Voorhis,
Mrs. Eleanor Wright.

POTOMAC SERIES is issued quarterly from 612 F street, Washington, D. C. Rhyme and Reason, No. 4, completes the first year, which will be furnished to annual subscribers for $1.00.

Back numbers furnished, post paid, for Twenty-five Cents.
Address 612 F street, Washington, D. C.